THE FOX WIFE'S TAIL

By Conrad Kinch

Copyright Conrad Kinch 2014

This book is available from Amazon.com

www.asimpleplanpress.com

A SIMPLE PLAN PRESS

This paperback edition published in 2017

Copyright © 2014 by Conrad Kinch

The moral right of the author has been asserted

All characters and events in this publication, other than those clearly in the public domain, are fictitious and any resemblance to real persons, living or dead, is purely coincidental.

All rights reserved.

No part of this publication may be reproduced, stored in a retrieval system, or transmitted, in any form or by any means, without the prior permission in writing of the publisher, nor be otherwise circulated in any form of binding or cover other that in which it is published and without a similar condition including this condition being imposed on the subsequent purchaser.

ISBN 978-1-53900-839-2

Designed and typeset in Lucida Bright
by Twistedinc Design, Dublin

www.asimpleplanpress.com

A Simple Plan Press

For my mother Clarissa

INTRODUCTION

This story has a beginning, as I suppose all stories must, with the truism that the world is a small place and getting smaller. It was the summer of 2005 and I was in my fifth year of wasting the very expensive education that my parents had gone to the trouble of buying for me. I had left college at the tender age of twenty having studied journalism with a plan of going abroad to the dirty wars of the twenty first century and becoming, in short, either dead or famous. My mother always told me that the key to getting ahead was liking yourself, that and a bit of determination. Talent was largely unimportant, any fool could have talent.

A four year long liaison with an American woman which had ended badly for both of us cured me at least of my desire to see myself "...dropped by a ten rupee jezzail" and so I stayed at home. I had entered a sort of career limbo in bookselling, which was dull, but comfortable. I was bothered enough to take care not to get myself fired, but not so industrious as to impinge greatly on my leisure or be promoted to a position where I might be called upon to do some work. I was (to the great distress of my mother) far too fastidious and cowardly for journalism as it is practised in Ireland, with its permanent amnesia and parade of half truths. I am by nature totally unsuited to journalism, mainly but not entirely, because I wouldn't know a newsworthy story if it bit me in the ass. However, one thing I do have an eye for, though I say so myself, is a good yarn. This, roughly speaking, is the same thing as a good story, but not quite.

And so I stayed, comfortable, bored and static.

Still, I was doing relatively well for myself, I was seeing my childhood sweetheart, my job kept me in books and I had a reasonable beginning at a career as a failed novelist. I tried to carry the whole thing off by not caring, supposing that if I didn't perhaps no-one else would. Suffice to say that when at the age of twenty five the tale you now hold in your hands, fell into mine, I had the time and inclination to make something of it. And like most good things that have come to me, it was a complete accident and down to the work of another.

My sweetheart, whom we shall call B to save her blushes, came from a long, though not entirely respectable line of actors. I was hoping to ask B to marry me, but I wasn't entirely sure she'd say yes. Modern woman is pretty gun-shy about the business. You have to prove yourself capable of being a provider, a good cook, thoughtful, a fine father, understanding, kind, strong, humourous and not least endlessly sexually inventive. And that's all before you ask her out for drinks.

All of this came as something of a shock to me, old romantic that I am, I'd supposed that you met the right girl, there was an embarrassed silence while you sounded each other out and then you just sort of turned up. However, once I'd realized what the initial hurdles consisted of, I decided the best course of action as to get B's mother M on side. Mothers are fond of weddings, there are hats to be thought of. And of course grandchildren, so I was starting with an advantage. So when M asked if could spare a couple of hours on Sunday morning to help her clear out her parents' basement I made loud cheery noises.

Now before we go any further, we should get one thing straight. I don't like dirt. Or dark places, or hard work or heavy lifting. I'm a fleshy young chap, B is kind enough to call me cuddly, but the fact of the matter is that I'm a fat bastard and getting hot, sweaty and unpleasant in someone else's basement is not my idea of a good time. Not that this mattered, faint heart never won fair lady. I mention it purely to illustrate the depth of my feeling and the sacrifices that I was prepared to make.

One of the consolations of cleaning the basement was that I got to spend time in the company of M's uncle, B's great uncle, who was also called M (that family never throws anything out, trust me, I've cleared their basement and this also applies to names), but who we shall call for clarity's sake M'uncle. M'uncle was a tiny, birdlike man, whose energy belied his eighty six years. He was that rare gem in this lousy modern world, a genuine eccentric. He collected with a passion; 19th century militaria, death masks, memorabilia of the mistresses of Napoleon III, old sheet music, celebrity wallpaper and shrapnel from the Great War. He divided his time amongst his army of female admirers (sadly platonic), redecorating the houses of family and friends (with or without their consent) and clearing the windows of the five storey pile that he shared with B's grandparents.

This he did as often as he could get away with it, dangling out of a top floor window, with a dressing gown cord lashed to the banisters and tied around his ankle, for "safety". He was perhaps the most anecdote worthy man I have ever met.

My favourite story about M'uncle, not least because I had dined out on it several times and because it, unlike many of my stories, had the virtue of being true, was about his most recent trip to Verdun. M'uncle had gone on his preferred holiday, a semi-annual trip to the old battlefields of France with a map, a flask of tea and a shovel. Late one day, towards the end of his trip, he was cycling happily down a small country lane on the way back to his hotel, the day's finds resting the front basket of his bicycle, when he saw a sinister looking guy in a bomber jacket running down the road after him. Unperturbed M'uncle quickened his pace somewhat only to see the guy break into a sprint. The runner began to yell, understandably enough, in French. M'uncle, despite his many visits, hasn't bothered to learn the language, having successfully made his way with gesture and shouting.

He was not a man to be intimidated by a young ruffian. So while still maintaining his dignity, he stood up on the pedals and accelerated. He was relieved when, five minutes later, he looked over his shoulder to see that he had lost his pursuer. He returned to his leisurely pace when the chap in the bomber jacket cleared the hedgerow that lined the lane, swept M'uncle from his bike and carried him bodily through the hedgerow opposite. The man, who on closer inspection turned out to be an off duty member of the local gendarmerie on his way home from a shift change, was soon standing M'uncle up and brushing him down. This young French policeman, filled perhaps with more compassion than sense, had spotted M'uncle from a distance some fifteen minutes before, loading his latest acquisition into the basket of his bicycle.

Terror does strange things to people, some people develop incredible strength under pressure while others simply go to pieces. I've never been entirely sure how the young gendarme was able to tell at a distance of nearly a hundred yards that what M'uncle was holding was in fact an unexploded seventy five millimeter shell, but the point is, for all concerned, that he did. An explosive ordnance disposal unit was called from the local army base and M'uncle's shell, bicycle, flask of tea and remaining sandwiches were made safe in a controlled explosion that rattled windows over a mile away.

But I digress. It was in the basement, and the company, of this extraordinary man that I spent several hours of a Sunday morning toting boxes of old newspapers, sweeping away long broken crockery, extricating myself from a tea chest of cockhorses that fell on my head and getting very dirty, sweaty and unpleasant. I also sneezed a great deal, my sinuses being of a particularly sensitive nature and likely to seize up completely at the least threat of hard work. It was during a pause in the morning's proceeding, when we had stopped for the third obligatory cup of tea, that I sat sneezing in the parlour idly leafing through a pile of cuttings charting the course of the Falklands war, that I found a packet.

It rested in my palm, about the size and shape of the large paperback book, wrapped neatly in yellow paper and tied with fraying, but still taut string. There were postcards tucked under the string, several sea-views, one a faded blue print of Mt. Fuji and the last a more recent addition, a Guinness advertisement, showing a Toucan making off with a pint. I looked down at the wrapping paper and felt a shiver of unreality pass through me. My nose felt suddenly clear and I gasped, I think I also swore. The postcards were blank and the latest, the one with the toucan, was from the early fifties, when my father was a boy. I squinted in the dim light of the parlour, holding the packet close, inhaling the heady aroma of dust, antiquity and old heavy paper. There it was still, a beautiful faded impossibility, delicate and spidery, but precise writing.

Papers. C. Kinch. 26 West Essex Street. 6th July 1889.

I'm not in the habit of addressing packets to myself. Especially when doing so would mean travelling back in time. I don't have the temperament.

Conrad had been my maternal grandfather's name, and it was unknown in my father's family. I was an aberration, a fact often remarked upon at family gatherings. I felt light headed and having stood up to put the postcards down and take a better look at the packet in the light.

M'uncle pottered loudly by, M had assembled boxes of rubbish to go in the skip that was arriving the next morning and M'uncle was importantly weeding them of all the things he absolutely couldn't do without, muttering to himself occasionally, "What would you be doing throwing that out?" And "Sure, I could fix that up for you no bother", when he saw me looking shocked and pale and sitting down in the parlour. He was definitely of the opinion that the younger generation wasn't made of particularly stern stuff, a fact not helped by the coincidence that I had first made his acquaintance while recovering from an operation for a double hernia. There are things more embarrassing than eighty six year old man who is concerned for your health, but I haven't encountered them.

Seeing that I was poorly or at least strangely quiet, he bustled over. There was an explosive of "By Jove!" by my elbow, followed a sotto voce "may I?", whereupon he lifted it up and stared at it, balancing the thing on the tips of small intelligent fingers. He removed his glasses and wiped his brow with a handkerchief, peering closer and then breathed out swiftly in two or three short hacking laughs.

"Ah, the Kinchs, of course, our old neighbours, from when they lived down the road. That chap must have been a," he paused "...a great, great, great, great, great?"

I had heard of these people before, Kinchs who'd lived on the street in days gone by. M had thought I was a descendant when first we'd met, but my family had moved into the city only recently. My father's family were from Clare, so that it was unlikely that the West Essex Street Kinchs were any relation. M'uncle had already begun to hold forth on "Kinchs I have known", when M stuck her head around the door to say that she was heading out Dun Laoghaire way and did I want a lift? She did this mainly, I suspect because she was always worried that I was listening to M'uncle out of politeness when I stayed to hear him on such diverse subjects as Garibaldi's barber and the sex life of Napoleon III. Nothing could have been further from the truth, M'uncle spoke with that rare gift, passion, I could listen to him for hours.

But today was different. I wanted that packet. I wanted it so badly, that the need was a pain in my chest, aching with each breath. I had to purposefully look at M to prevent myself from staring at it. I couldn't think of a way to get at it, honestly at least, and as these were my friends, hopefully my perspective in-laws, simply taking it was out of the question. But the need was nagging and being near the thing frustrating, so I nodded that I would go, just to be away from it. B was out in Dun Laoghaire anyway and perhaps I could intrigue with her to get it some-how.

M'uncle wished us goodbye with a bemused expression and the packet hanging in his right hand while I went and grabbed my coat. I was standing behind M as she wrestled with the variety of Victorian locks, when M'uncle bounded up the stairs and pushed the packet in my hands. The paper felt rough like raw silk beneath my finger tips. I murmured a stunned "thank you" and realized that I'd never contradicted him about my being a Clare rather than a Dublin Kinch. I tried to say it, but my dry throat just croaked. M'uncle brushed this off with a wide smile and said, "Render unto Caesar the things that are Caesar's" and then I was in the passenger seat of M's tiny car, my knees neatly framing my face and the smell of old paper and old stories heady in the air.

And so a small enterprise was begun, with what I hope was a small sin, which I have since confessed to and been absolved of, but which I committed all the same.

Conrad Kinch 12th July 2005

PHOTOGRAPHIC PLATES

Undated portrait of Captain Robert Hood. Believed to have been painted circa 1855-1857. My thanks to the Hood family for their kind permission to use this photograph.

Sword believed to have been the property of Captain Robert Hood. The hilt bears British markings and it is said by family legend that the sword came into his possession during his travels in Italy.

Map of the Empire of Japan. Circa 1850.

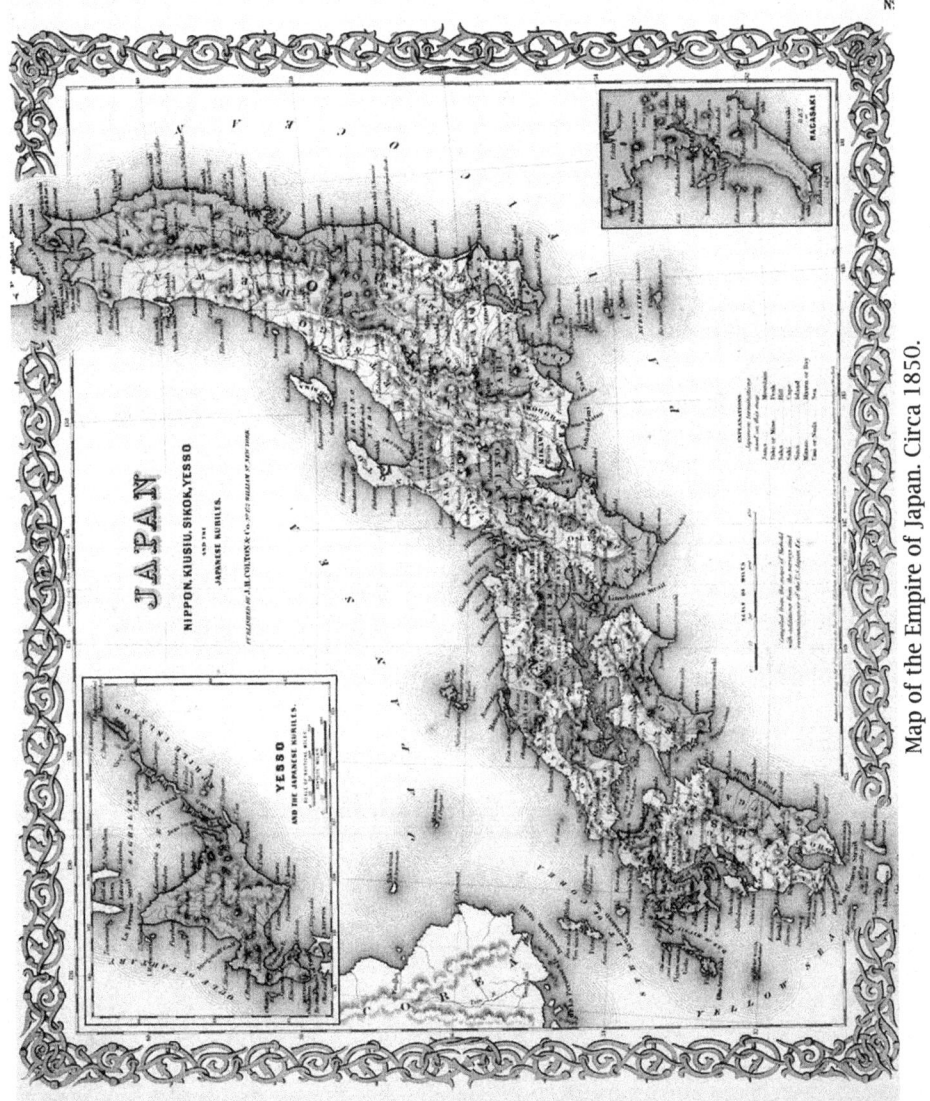

Castle Of Blood

or

THE FOX WIFE'S TAIL

A Tale of Old Nippon

As transcribed in May of 1860
by Conrad Patrick Kinch of Dublin from
the testimony of Brevet Major Robert Hood,
Second United States Dragoons and
edited for publication by Conrad Kinch, 2005.

1

A discovery and introductions.

He had fought like a lion. The footsteps in the dust showed it. Twirling, whirling marks circling like dancers, here a spot of dark blood, there a pause and then a turn and again the feet were moving. Otaro crouched, hunched in the peculiar oriental way, reading the steps like a man surveying a map for the first time. His hands tucked into his sleeves, his lips moving soundlessly, reading what I could see but not understand. That one had fought against many, that I could fathom, the ring of footsteps around him growing smaller as the wolves closed, the mark of a body falling showing they had strayed too close, a splash of blood; the sign that the lion was weakening.

Otaro was short, even for a Japanese, an effect more pronounced by the hunch with which he faced the world. His robe was drawn tight over the paunch that told of good living. He looked like a farmer, prosperous in a small way, who like to laugh and eat and take such simple pleasures as came by. But this impression was belied by his eyes, which were big and soft and brown, but carried within them the seeds of a ruthless determination, twinkling with laughter at one moment and then gazing at you with the pitiless hunger of a crocodile the next.

His swords, which were so much his constant companions that they were almost part of the man, they had the longest grips that I had seen on a weapon in Japan, where swords are worn openly and at all times. It was explained to me that these were ancestral blades, of antique vintage, crafted in a time when swords were more often used. These days, hilts were made shorter so that the weapon was easier to sit with.

"Longer handle cuts better," Otaro had said and refused to be drawn further on the matter.

But I bore you with details.

So there we were standing amidst the aftermath of a battle and no clue as to how or why it had occurred. I looked out over the valley, watching the people, specks in the distance returning home from the fields at days end, while Otaro paced back and forth, the wind stirred a little.

The death of the porters that I could understand. The wind had been before us and had not carried the stench of offal, but we had heard the flies. Six men, young and fit, in pale green livery, all cut down from behind as they had tried to carry their charge away. The paper walls of the sedan chair gaped like broken eggshell where the passenger had been thrown clear. Entrails glistened and spines gleamed whitely at us in the dying light of the day. Men in armour, their lacquered breastplates showing the same heraldic design as the porters livery lay back to back, dead by their spears.

They had been surrounded, but not immediately overwhelmed. Their attackers' chief object was the chair. I joined Otaro at his study.

"How many at the chair?"

"A dozen maybe. Some delayed the guards, while the others killed the porters".

Otaro pointed to a mark in the dust.

"He was thrown and dropped something," he touched the dust, "here. And ran to it. He did not draw until he'd reached it."

I followed the steps in the dirt as best I could, feeling like a youth at his first dance lesson. I can read a man's footwork well enough when it is in front of me, but divining it from footsteps in the dust is not something I have had much call for.

"And they surrounded him?"

Otaro nodded.

"He used the two handed style, but fought with only one hand."

How he could fathom that I could not tell, but listened, the gist was becoming clear to me now and I kept silent for fear of saying something stupid.

"He slew three. Was wounded four times in return. Never fatally. Each time in the back."

Otaro was circling the ground, his legs set wide, crouching, his head dipping to scrutinize some detail.

"And then ran. This way," he motioned towards the edge of the road or track as it would more properly be called.

Even as we walked to the edge of the track I felt doubt growing in me. Could Otaro really read the dust so completely? Though my friend was counted amongst the greatest swordsmen in the land, I was not sure. I have seen savage redskins read a trail with a facility that would astonish a civilized man, but even so I thought that Otaro must be putting forth at least some bluff.

At the lip of the road, looking down the valley turned red by the setting sun, we crept forward. The edge of the track was mere feet away from a sheer drop of some fifty or sixty feet. I have never liked heights and the sight of my friend craning his head over the edge was enough to flutter my stomach. But not to be outdone, I steeled myself, hoping my younger keener eyes might spot something that he had missed.

"He jumped," said Otaro simply and tucked his hands into his sleeves again. The vision of leaping into that horribly empty drop made my head swim. But I recovered myself.

There was a man lying beneath us on a ledge, his kimono green with dark patches. Broken branches marked a path to where he had fallen and his head was at an unnatural angle. I called to Otaro and felt a little satisfaction at his flicker of irritation. He sat at the edge of the drop, watching for several minutes.

Retreating from the stomach churning sight, I walked around the site again, pleased as punch and hoping to find some other clue that my friend might have missed. When I returned, he was back at the place where the initial melee had occurred.

"They were definitely samurai," I opined, hefting a spear shaft that I had taken from one of the guards. It was cut straight through. I have had cause to defend myself with a spear, in fact a flagstaff, and blades typically cut slivers from such a weapon.

Otaro turned and looked at me, I could almost see the surprise behind his mask of eastern inscrutability.

"Definitely samurai, I'd stake a years pay on it. Look at that. Only a samurai blade wielded by a very powerful man could have inflicted such a cut."

He nodded and smiled, obviously pleased with the extra information.

"So it's war then. And not merely banditry?" He nodded.

"We must search for nine men. All fine swordsmen. Three of whom trained in Satsuma. One under Master Itcho in Edo. The others are Takeda. Or trained by them. They fight as men more used to horseback. Three Takedas fell. None were poor fighters. But he was better and for them it was deadly ground."

He settled his swords in his belt and turned on his heel. I stood and thought on this, then ran after him, the words tumbling from my mouth.

"Three? Three of them fell? The Takedas? I see no drag marks, where are the bodies?"

Otaro continued up the road.

"Where indeed, Captain Robert?"

And it was thus that we continued our journey to the castle.

I suppose I should pause a moment in my narrative, so that my reader may know all the facts. I shall start with a brief biographical sketch of my friend. Otaro was the youngest son of a minor noble house. He was unusual amongst the Japanese in that he had no family, having been orphaned in early manhood by a massive fire that claimed mother, father and all his brothers and sisters besides. He had been raised in the household of his fencing master, an old and trusted family retainer. It was under this benefactor's roof that his talents as a swordsman blossomed.

Even as a young man he garnered much recognition for his skill in this field, as excellence in fencing is very highly thought of in Japan, so much that great men vied to study under him and is was thought to be a great thing to have taken a lesson with him. Thus it was that he came to instruct albeit briefly, the Pope[1] of Japan. Though I heard in the cantonment that his current post, that of a wandering magistrate, was secured for him by a political rival who wished to separate him from the Pope.

---

[1] Here Captain Robert means the Emperor, often referred to as the Pope by westerners during this period because while he was a supreme spiritual leader of the nation, temporal power rested with the Shogun (also known at the Tai-Kun or Tycoon).

I, myself, am of no great moment. I was born in Boston, my people being merchants who dealt in coffee and tea. As a youth I attended West Point military academy, and as I was no mathematician I failed to secure the posting to the topographical engineers that my father had wished for me. I was instead commissioned into the cavalry. Service in the mounted arm was no hardship for me as I have always loved horses, and it offered plenty of opportunity for action though only against redskins. It was there that I picked up the smattering of Navaho, Apache and Coo-man-chee that I have. I saw service in the war against Mexico, being promoted Captain and finally a Brevet Major for my part of the affair at Vera Cruz.

Sadly, peace time soldiering and the sudden arrival at my post of a commanding officer as barbarous as the savages we were meant to keep in check soured me on the army and I resigned. Having no employment, I wandered a little[2], but was eventually commissioned by a group of my father's friends to spend a year in Japan, which had lately been opened up to trade by the good offices of Commodore Perry[3]. It was thought that my experience in dealing with the savage peoples of the west would suit me to exploring the commercial opportunities offered by the decadent, yet no less savage peoples of the east.

---

2 Though exactly where is hard to tell, Captain Hoods service record states that he resigned his commission on the 9th of September 1856. To the best of my knowledge his last descendant died in 1963, his papers donated to the city. Thanks to the kind help of Boston local historian, Dr. Heather Wiencko, I have been able been able to peruse photocopies of several family documents, one of which refers to an "Uncle Bob" who traveled widely "...in Europe and the Orient". One surviving letter, dated May 1857, indicates that Captain Hood did spend some time in Paris in the spring of that year.

3 Perry, Matthew C. (1794-1858) U.S. naval officer who headed an expedition that forced Japan in 1853-54 to enter into trade and diplomatic relations with the West after more than two centuries of isolation.

Languages have always been a forte of mine. I have Spanish, Italian, Latin, a little Greek from my mother, French from the academy and such redskin dialects as I learned on service. I found the tongue relatively easy to pick up, though its subtle courtesies often eluded me. I spent two months in Yokuhama[4], learning much of the language, but frustratingly little of the country. I knew that to venture into the interior would mean death at the hands of vengeful samurai who resented our arrival. Otaro was introduced to me by a mutual acquaintance as one of the Japanese warrior class who wished to learn about his American counterparts. I proposed a trade. I would teach him about the armies of the West, if he would allow me to accompany him on his travels.

It proved a strange partnership indeed.

---

4 Yokohama, one of the few ports open to Europeans at this date. It must be remembered that there was no standard manner of spelling Japanese in the roman alphabet at this date, hence Captain Robert's references to Yokoohama, Yukahama, Yeddo, Jedoo and Osaca. I've simply used the first spelling given throughout.

2

*The Castle.
Sad news of a child.
An unfortunate case of nerves in the night.*

It was late when we reached the castle and the setting sun turned it a deep red, as if the landscape all around were drenched with blood. The castle itself had that queer, fairy tale look of eastern fortresses, the brightly coloured pagodas rising above squat stone work like hovering butterflies. It was almost dark when Otaro knocked at the door and it was only after lengthy discussion, and after our papers had been examined, we were admitted. The guards were shocked to see me. I suppose I was the first white man the simple fellows had ever laid eyes upon, but after a moment's commotion they regained their composure and assumed again the stoic countenance that is the mark of the Japanese.

I suppose I should pause for a moment and explain the state of affairs in Japan, a country that is a mystery to most and I must confess, despite my time there, is still largely a mystery to me.

Japan is an archipelago, south of the Russian Empire and east-north-east of China, though with a people and culture much closer to the latter than the former. Its people are wholly Asiatic and are divided into two castes, peasants and noblemen. As in feudal times in England, all noblemen, also called samurai, are expected to be in training for war and wear swords as a mark of their exalted rank. This noble caste choose from amongst their ranks a king or Tycoon, whose appointment is then approved by the pope of Japan, also known as the son of heaven. This appointment is an uncertain one, as the noblemen of Japan are like medieval barons of Europe, constantly squabbling, and so to prevent revolt, it is the custom for noblemen to spend half the year in the capital.

Until recently Japan was closed to outsiders, baring a few Dutch traders, because of the prejudices of the Pope, who disdained foreigners. It was not until Commodore Perry of the United States Navy met with the Tycoon several years ago, that Japan opened it's doors to trade. The Japanese, though not civilized, are an orderly people and while there are elements that abhor foreigners, for the most part the Tycoons edicts have been obeyed.

A servant brought us clothes and water that we might wash the dust of the road from us and then we were brought before the butler of the castle, an old gentleman called Yoshi. He was an old man and immensely thin and his large head with its heavy lidded eyes watched us as we entered, balanced on an inordinately long neck, so that he appeared like a crane. Otaro made the introductions. My Japanese, though serviceable, was crude enough to give offence to those not used to it.

The butler enquired after our business and Otaro replied that he was a magistrate, travelling north to adjudicate in a land dispute, that I was his companion and that we had come seeking food and shelter, but also that we had grave news of murder committed on the road.

"What is the murder of which you speak?" asked the butler. He and Otaro had, I think, taken a dislike to each other and were speaking formally, so that I could barely make it out.

"A noble man, his bearers and guards were taken in ambush some hours ago. They were all killed. The attackers knew their business. I would suspect your Lord is amongst the dead. Am I correct?"

"Lord Hoji has travelled to a shrine in the mountains to thank the gods for the birth of his new son. He will be back shortly." The butler stammered.

"Then of course, it is so," said Otaro and set his shoulders. He seemed embarrassed by the man's distress.

"But you are hungry and must eat," the butler said, rising quickly. And as his words died away, I heard a humming rising all about me. It was soft and low, a susurration of many voices all speaking at once, quiet but urgent, the waxing of an underground stream. Otaro and the butler paid it no heed, but I suddenly realized that the paper walls around us concealed people. I became uncomfortable and started trying to spot shadows against the pearlescent white of the walls.

The butler left us and other servants came and we were brought to other rooms, through a garden of breathtaking beauty. I had not been more than six weeks in Japan, so it could not have been more than late March, but the trees were heavy with soft white blossom, crouching queerly over still pools that mirrored them amidst a field of stars.

Our room overlooked the garden and I found it hard to tear my eyes from it as we were greeted by a diminutive lady who took our swords from us and placed them on a rack. She was small, little bigger than a child and to me she seemed like a porcelain doll given life. Her pale, almost translucent, skin seemingly devoid of paint bar a violent slash of red across her mouth. Her dress was neat and her movement was delicacy itself, so that I felt as if in the presence of an automaton. Having struggled a little with the weight of my sabre, she was brought boxes by another girl, who seemed only slightly more real than her fellow. From the boxes were produced rice and fish, which we ate while our hostess brewed the astringent green tea that I had grown used to during my stay. All this she did without words. Once we had supped, she and her companion gathered together all that they had brought. But there was a backwards glance that caught my friends eye and both he and the lady gazed fixedly at each other for a moment.

"Is my husband dead, magistrate[5]?" She asked simply.

---

[5] It is unclear what title is being referred to here. While almost all magistrates were samurai, they were like the majority of samurai in Japan at that time, warriors in name only and were accompanied by a large retinue of followers. That Otaro has legal powers of some sort is clear, but, the idea of a magistrate wandering in the manner of a US Marshall is not known in Japan. It is unlikely that Otaro was actually a magistrate in the accepted sense. Given his powerful friends, his post was probably a special one, created specifically for him. My thanks to Mr. Fintan Hoey for this information.

"Yes, my lady."

"And the child?"

"I do not know."

"Goodnight, gentlemen."

And with that she left.

Though there had been meaning in their words that I did not catch, those parts that I did understand startled me. I was filled with a burning curiosity and hurried to ask Otaro to tell me all. He shook his head and said that he would go for a walk in the garden. I would have joined him but I thought that after the events of the day he would prefer to be alone.

As I sat there, I heard a great clamor, running and shouting and the familiar rattle of saddle and tack. Horses were being prepared, at least half a dozen by the sound and I stepped to the wooden porch of our chamber to see men running hither and thither in the darkness. One man, young and huge for Japanese, clad in the full battle armour of a samurai mounted his horse and dismissing his attendant with a kick, thundered out of the castle, his followers at his heels.

Otaro indicated with a grunt, that the departing warrior was the murdered man's son, out for revenge. Watching him ride out brought home to me the truth that to live in Japan is to brush shoulders with men whose world is that of Sir. Walter Scott's novels. Theirs is a crude chivalry, with nothing of gentility about it, but it is chivalry nonetheless.

I was sitting in our chamber turning things over in my head when Otaro returned and said that it would be well if we slept. He unrolled mats that had been left for the purpose and I pillowed my head on the thin bolster and stared up at the rafters above me.

"Captain Robert," he spoke softly in the darkness.

"Yes."

"This is a very bad business. I doubt things will be jolly good soon."

He had switched to English, his command of which was slightly better than my Japanese.

"Are we being spied upon?"

"In the normal way. No more. We are not under suspicion."

"So it is murder then."

"That or war. Most likely murder. The neighbouring Lord and Lord Hoji have not been on the best of terms for many years. The Pope himself knows it."

"You think it an attack by this other fellow? And what of the child? What is going on, Otaro?"

"That cannot be seen for the present. I doubt it is this Lord Ite. There has been no formal application for vendetta. Also, to command twelve such men as attacked the procession would be beyond his pockets. The child is Lord Hoji's newborn son. The child of the lady you just met."

"Then who is the other fellow, the furious one, who just left? He and the lady must be of an age."

"He is Lord Hoji's nephew and heir, son of his elder brother, Saigo. Saigo was killed in ambush by Lord Ite. There was a feud years ago. It was very bloody. It was by Saigo's death that Lord Hoji got his title and he proclaimed that his brother's son would inherit."

"And this new son?"

"Who can say? Lord Hoji had him at his side during the fight. Fought one handed because of it."

I thought on this and then asked a question of Otaro, which plainly irritated him as he was near slumber.

"But if these twelve were the warriors you say they are, why did they find one man so difficult to overcome?"

"Lord Hoji was a swordsman of note. He studied under Master Sum. Master Sum retired here some years ago."

"This Sum, is he good? Do you know him?"

"Yes, but only by his deeds. He is very good. Good night, Captain Robert."

And with that he rolled over and slept. I lay there a long time thinking. My mind racing. There had been no child lying by the Lord's body. He might have fallen, but it seemed unlikely. The father who leapt from the cliff edge would not have let his son slip from his grasp. Thus the child might have been taken or have secreted himself in some crack or crevice. I set my mind to recovering the boy, regardless of the consequences. Otaro would be required to stay on to investigate the murder. The land question was not a pressing concern. We would find men and ropes in the morning, of that I was sure. But then my thoughts turned to darker thing. Lord Hoji's nephew was the heir, what position would the new son put him in? I knew little of the customs of succession here, but as I drowsed, grim dreams danced in my head of Richard the Third and the Princes in the tower, a small child falling into emptiness and his cousin dressed in all war's barbaric panoply.

I slept fitfully, turning often and waking with a start some time after midnight. I felt suddenly alert and held myself taut in the darkness, I could hear Otaro breathing low and regular to my left. What had woken me? The black of night was total though slowly my eyes grew accustomed to the darkness and I began to perceive the beams above faintly caught in the dim moonlight filtering through paper.

There was a noise, almost imperceptible, a scratching and I tensed again. I held my breath hoping to catch it. There it was again, slow, tentative, but definitely there. I lay completely still my breath as deep as I dared and there again was the scratching.

Over my head.

I studied the beams intently and let my hands slip to my belt where my revolver was holstered. There was a low moan from Otaro and seizing the moment I unbuttoned the holster under cover of his noise. Who could the intruder be? Not a spy surely?

An assassin perhaps? Had Lord Hoji's nephew decided that a magistrate on the premises was an unacceptable risk? I held my gaze steady on the roof above, studying then eliminating those shadows that might conceal a man. On the roof then. It was not the scrape of feet on ceramic that I had heard, but there it came again, another soft scratching and then a panting sound from the eaves of the chamber furthest from me.

Otaro moaned again, then grunted and rolled over in slumber. I thanked God for my sleeping friends noise and quickly slipped my gun from its case. Suddenly Otaro rolled over again and cast an arm over my chest, trapping my gun beneath his body. I barely stopped myself from shouting in surprise. I struggled to cock my gun, but to no avail. I have slept in close proximity with men before as one does to keep warm on campaign, but I grew very disconcerted when my friend began to nuzzle into my neck.

I paused, trying to slow my breathing and cursing my luck. The luck that meant that my friend, who normally slumbered as quietly as the dead, had made enough noise to cover my freeing my pistol, but that almost meant that he should choose this night to toss in his bedclothes and land me in the predicament I found myself in. Resolving that I could at least roll Otaro off swiftly if the need arose, I turned my eyes to the darkness under the eave again. But it could not be, no man, not even a child could conceal themselves in the shadows there. It was impossible, but yet the noise came from there.

I stared upwards, willing the darkness to part, but succeeded only in straining my eyes. They ached with the exertion and began to droop. The tension in my body was dissipating and the warmth of my friend against me began to exercise a soporific effect. I fought against it, blinking and staring ever more fixedly into the shadows and yet even as I struggled, my lids dropped and my body began to relax until I blinked.

And awoke with a start.

My hand was on my pistol ready to cock it, but Otaro was not there. I rolled and saw his sleeping form some feet away from me. I lay stiff with tension for several minutes my nerves like whipcord, berating myself for having drowsed when I should have been on my guard. But there were no more mysterious noises and finally sleep claimed me.

3

*A return to the killing ground.
Thoughts on labourers and undertakers.
A mystery.*

We rose early, before even the bright sunlight had entered our chamber and we washed and dressed. Otaro took longer then was usual at his toilet, so that I stood alone for a few minutes on the porch overlooking the stable and the castle gates. The murdered Lord's nephew, the next Lord Hoji I supposed, had arrived as we were washing and was remonstrating with his stableboy, an elderly Japanese, who cringed before the bellowing ruffian, his wispy beard swaying like Spanish moss as he bobbed and bowed.

Otaro joined me and sitting on the porch we planned the orders of the day. We agreed that returning to the fallen Lord and recovering his body, as well as finding the child were the matters of first import. With that object in mind Otaro approached Lady Hoji to gain the services of some stout men and strong ropes. I passed to the opposite porch which faced the garden and offered the more pleasant view. I sat a while in the Japanese fashion, modified to take account of American trousers and waited for the servants, who were in our chamber, to depart, as I was determined as soon as I unobserved to study the rafters where I supposed the intruder, had lain in wait.

I was biding my time when I was distracted by the sight of an oldish man of middle height, dressed in a kimono of powder blue, striding into the garden from the chamber adjacent to my own. He had a lean rangy figure and had in the wiry cast of his frame and the set of his countenance that air of self possession and strength that distinguishes our frontiersmen. He carried with him a booken or wooden practice sword used by samurai in their exercise. Pulling one arm free of his robe and tying the remainder tight about him, he took up a Japanese fencing stance by the pond. I was used to this. I had seen it before, the samurai at their fencing practice all turning and shouting in unison like recruits on a barracks square.

It soon became clear though that this was a man of an entirely different sort. Unlike the regimented samurai, he was a tiger, silent and terrible. He struck blows, counters and cuts with superhuman rapidity, turning, slashing in each direction. These were not the manic slashes of a panicked man, each one stopped just so and the blade turned to another. I watched, engrossed. Surely this must be the Master Sum of whom Otaro had spoken. He was the man who had taught the fallen lion of yesterday, one man standing against many like a whirling, but disciplined, dervish.

He stopped and held his weapon at his side. I forgot all else and clapped with admiration, at which he started, then turned towards me and bowed. I scrambled to my feet and returned his courtesy. Tucking the wooden sword into his girdle, he walked towards me and I bowed again, low as I had been taught to when meeting a person of quality. He returned my bow with a slight gesture of respect as one might make to a guest, he turned on his heel and left.

And that was my introduction to the eccentric fencing master, Master Sum.

I was still standing agape when Otaro returned. He looked at me quizzically, but asked no question, informing me only that such men and ropes as were needed had been got and that we had best be off. The air was crisp and cool as we began our march back to the place of slaughter, and I must confess I was so taken with the beauty about me that I quite forgot the reason for our errand. The valley sides, lush and green, towered over us like the nave of a great cathedral, villages and rice fields dotted with industrious peasants were revealed to us as the bright sun burned off the early morning mist. It was, I suppose, about seven o'clock by the time we reached the killing ground. I had become lost in the study of my surroundings and had been humming a jaunty little tune when we caught the stench of death on the air. We had with us two dozen men, good sturdy fellows, compact, but strong of limb and blessed with the tremendous self possession and good humoured cheerfulness that marks the Japanese peasant in the pursuit of his duty.

Eighteen of the fellows were family retainers, while the other six were funeral attendants brought specially for the purpose. The retainers had precedence it seemed and were first behind us in the column of march, a fact which was established after much bowing and scraping on the part of the morticians. I gave it little thought, though it brought a sudden homesick pang to my chest for the more egalitarian manners of my homeland.

What was stranger still was the appearance of the scene of the previous days outrage. Though flies still buzzed about the slain, there were no marks of scavengers at all. Even queerer to my mind was the absence of hoof marks, Lord Hoji's heir having obviously not troubled himself to visit the site of his step father's end.

Otaro directed our assistants with curt words of command and nods of the head and the boys assembled two harnesses suspended on ropes. Fear plucked at my heart and I believe I may have been trembling, but as ever in man, pride pushed me where courage could not and I joined Otaro in one of the harnesses. With a sickening push into emptiness, during which I had my eyes firmly shut, we were lowered swinging wildly to the ledge.

Opening my eyes, I found myself on my knees in the dirt and face to face with Lord Hoji. His head was thrown back and his teeth bared in a snarl that showed defiance even in the end. That his neck was turned around on his shoulders at an impossible angle and his face discoloured by a dark pulpy mark only underlined his tenacity.

He was tall for a Japanese, broad, with a full, deep chest, strong sinewy arms and the thick wrists of a swordsman. Though a man of middle years, he was obviously still well in training. His jaw was strong and his brow dark, his samurai tonsure exposing a large cranium which spoke of intelligence and good sense. The simplicity of his dress marked him as a man of taste and culture. But always my gaze returned to the bared teeth and the blazing eyes. This was a tiger at bay, terrible even in death.

Otaro was on all fours beside me studying the ground, while I observed the fallen man. There was no sign of the child. The ledge was small barely eight feet by four and Otaro and I were crowded because of it. I knew enough of the taboos about touching dead flesh to search Lord Hoji's corpse, but was considering turning him over, when Otaro grabbed me and bade me be still. Reaching between my feet he picked up a small ivory token bound with a cord like a baby's rattle and then asked me to edge back a few inches. Pointing where I squatted he traced his fingers through the earth and bare stone.

"See here? The child has lain here. He cannot yet crawl. But he is not here now."

I was quiet for a moment, I knew little of the fauna of Japan, but even in the wilds of the Texas, buzzards are not capable of carrying off entire children. I was about to ask if a bird of prey unknown to me could have been responsible, when Otaro held up his hand again.

"The sword also lay here. Hilt there." He indicated with a thumb.

A sickening thought rose in my breast. Otaro looked at me and without thinking I blurted it out.

"Could perhaps the Lord with his dying breath, fearing the capture and disgrace of his son and ancestral blade have pushed them from the edge?" The samurai of Japan are known for their superhuman sensitivity to slight, yet I hesitated to consider one capable of infanticide.

"Unlikely," said Otaro, "the marks do not support it. Also Captain Robert, that man's neck is broken. Snapped instantly when he hit his head, dead men do not often push people from cliffs. But there is one way to be sure."

He drew a cord from his sleeve and looping it, passed it over the dead man's wrist and bracing himself against the cliff face, he heaved, rolling the body over. It turned, the head flopping at a sickening angle, baring the front drenched in blood and cut many times, some to the bone.

Otaro sighed, "He fought one handed because he was holding his son. Yet regard his girdle." I did and saw nothing stranger than the fact that it was soaked in blood. I turned questioningly to my friend.

"There is no scabbard there. No short sword either. There is no sign that he dropped either above and the ground here has not been disturbed."

His voice trailed off and he dipped his head suddenly, closely regarding the earth by the fallen man. He frowned and furrowed his brow and I impatiently leaned forward to see.

There in the dust, on a ledge on a sheer cliff, where nothing could reach unless it had ropes or the power of flight was a small, perfectly formed impossibility. And yet there is was some two inches long and as sharp and clear as if it had been made moments before.

The clear and definite print of a paw.

4

The return to the castle.
A most unsatisfactory audience.
A walk in the garden and some unpleasant news.

We waited. The undertakers, working apart from the other men, had gathered the bodies together in rows, wrapping each in cloth. Otaro stood at the edge of the precipice looking out at the fields below, while I watched the undertakers at their work. Once each body was wrapped, they were slung across poles brought for the purpose, two bearers to a body.

I had noticed that Otaro had destroyed the paw print before the bearers had hauled us up and the undertakers were lowered down to retrieve the body of their fallen Lord. I sat at the road's edge, smoking, until the bearers were ready, their loads hanging like silk cocoons of spiders from a branch. Otaro took the lead as we trudged back to the castle, our pace, slow but steady in deference to the bearers, sweating beneath their loads.

We walked a while in silence, Otaro his posture erect, chest thrust out, his swords pressed flat against his paunch. My mind was full of speculation. Who could have taken both swords and child without leaving a trace or even a sign of having covered a trail? The paw print was a sign, a message of some sort, what would have been called amongst the simple backwoods folk of Maine, my mother's country, a hex sign. I was reminded of the Lamb's Tales of Shakespeare of my youth. Lady Macbeth crying of the damned spot that marked her as a murderess and the shivering nights of terror she had given me, her and her indelible mark of guilt.

Otaro had forced the pace somewhat at one of the inclines and the line was straggling, so that we were some dozen yards ahead of the others. I was about to speak when he did so, not turning to look at me, but speaking English quietly, swallowing his R's and W's even more so than usual.

"Captain Robert, please do not look around and do please keep your voice down. There is a man listening behind us, though I doubt they speak English."

I nodded an assent.

"The child was taken then, and the swords as well?"

"Indeed, Captain Robert, that is so."

"And the impression of the paw, is it a mark of some kind, a message perhaps? Is it a sign of a secret society or some such?"

At that Otaro inclined his head to me imperceptibly and regarded me, pursing his lips as if I had made a joke in poor taste.

"I think not, but I am not from this province and I suppose it is possible."

"Then perhaps the ambush was the work of such a society and not Lord Ide. Shall we expect the boy to be ransomed at least?"

"You are very concerned about the child, Captain Robert."

Now it was my turn to look surprised, though I struggled to mask my emotions, aware of the footsteps behind us. It seemed a singularly cold blooded statement, particularly as I knew that Otaro, like most Japanese was very fond of children and allowed them a license that would have been unheard of in America.

"I sincerely hope that he is alive and that we shall find him, you think it unlikely that he will be ransomed?"

"I hope that the boy is alive. His cousin is to be the new Lord."

"You suspect him," I asked, "of hurrying along his inheritance?"

"It seems unlikely. He is not a bad fellow, but." He left the sentence trail off and then began again, "...would you pay a ransom for a child who might complicate your inheritance?'

Indeed, I might not, I thought, even if I had nothing to do with the sudden arrival of that inheritance. We trudged on, the sun rising at our back and, not for the first time, I regretted acquiescing to Otaro's insistence that we travel on foot. As a cavalryman, I have a natural aversion to shanks mare[6], though I had yet another reason to thank my friend, Hugo Sinclair, late of the infantry and veteran of many a forced march, for his advice that I replace my fine English riding boots with a sturdy pair of common brogans[7].

---
6 A slang term meaning to walk on foot.
7 A type of tough walking shoe.

As we neared the castle, Otaro sent a runner ahead to announce our coming, and as we turned a bend in the road, I saw the castle for the first time in bright daylight. The queer fairytale look of the night before was even more pronounced now as the walls were hung with huge white banners marked with the curious picture writing peculiar to the orient. Banners also hung vertically from poles, suspended there in the manner of a Roman eagle. These were hung with streamers. The entire effect, the bright white shining in the glare of noon, was strangely ethereal as if the castle had been hung with mirrors. The impression of unreality, imposing though it was, did not draw my attention away from the other change, the posting of guards on the walls. They were watching discretely shaded by straw hats and hidden in the lee of towers and behind the larger banners. The new Lord clearly expected trouble.

We passed through the gates guarded by smartly turned out young samurai bearing spears, to find the courtyard a bustle. There were carpenters working, samurai at their exercise and over a dozen attendants, whom I did not recognize, chatting or holding horses.

"Who are they?" I asked Otaro.

"Servants from the families of the men who were killed. The samurai at least. The commoners are over there." He indicated a small group of women and children sitting quietly in the shadow of the castle walls. There were several old men with them. They were a pathetic sight, waiting timidly in their simple peasant's blue. Several of the children began to cry when the bodies were carried in. The women hushed them, regarding us quietly. It was a look I'd seen before in the eyes of Mexican peons, after their livestock had been taken or their children killed by stray bullets. It was stoic, not indifferent, but comprehending a hard life marked by the vicissitudes of fate. Their capacity for suffering was admirable, yet chilling also.

A priest was stumbling between the bodies, muttering, pausing only to fling quantities of salt about. Otaro and I were caught by one of these, at which I took great offence, declining to take the matter further only after Otaro assured me that the priests action had been to cleanse us. Which was all very well, but I can't say I took being pelted with salt gracefully.

We were greeted in the yard, by the butler, whom I had discovered was called Ittei. He regarded us nervously I thought, and I noticed that he was dressed entirely in white, as were the other servants that I saw. He bowed and we returned the bow.

"You have recovered my masters body?" he asked, licking his lips. Otaro nodded to the bearers who, carrying the corpse on a stretcher to distinguish it from the common dead, were standing in the yard waiting for instructions. He excused himself and walked to them, addressing them in an imperious manner to convey their Lord's and the other bodies to the undertakers on the other side of the castle. I looked at Otaro and he shrugged, while the butler returning to us smiled and said.

"Lord Hoji wishes to speak with you." Otaro nodded and we were led into the castle itself, past the visitors quarters where we had spent the night and through two narrow gates. More servants passed through the gates watched by samurai in sun hats, some of whom seemed little used to sentry go[8] and were glowing with sweat, even in the comparative cool of the castle interior. They too, were in white, the crisp fabric of their kimonos bright like bone in the sun.

I leaned closer to Otaro.

"Why are they all dressed in white?"

"Mourning dress," he replied and with that we entered the chamber of the new Lord.

The room was large, and the new Lord Hoji stood with several advisers at the rear of room. The walls had been moved to make it larger and the doors drawn back to admit air and permit a view of a curious garden. The men were kneeling around a pile of maps and papers, a clerk taking dictation at one side, we halted as the butler announced us and bowed. Having no idea as to the new Lord's station or whether he even was the new Lord, I copied Otaro, bowing low and holding the position until the courtesy was returned with an inclination of the head.

Though as a free-born American brought up to believe in the ideals of freedom and equality as borne out by the old fellows during the Revolution, I always found these displays of deference embarrassing. I took them as a regrettable part of daily life here and sometimes amused my self by imagining that I was bowing to a lady. Moreover, one must be pragmatic and though the

---

8 Sentry go – an old term for sentry duty.

murder of Americans is harshly punished by our navy, that is no comfort to one who has been beheaded by a slighted samurai. Thus in Japan it is sometimes necessary to bow your head so as to keep it.

These formalities done with, we advanced and sat at the places Ittei indicated for us.

The new Lord Hoji, seemed no less imposing out of armour than he had the night before. His advisors, who were four in number, were, excepting Master Sum, younger men, none of them older than myself. Dressed scrupulously in white, two of them had gone so far as to use some form of face powder to make their countenances even paler. Their decoration had not stopped there, as they had also rouged their lips so enthusiastically that they looked as if they had been battening on raw meat. The effect should have been ridiculous, but was somehow threatening, more like a Coomanchee in his paint and war bonnet than a lady with her face made up for the evening. I noticed, even as we sat, that all the men were wearing swords with long handles.

The conversation was rapid and all in Japanese, I followed to the best of my ability and Otaro would occasionally pause to translate, which I noted, irritated Lord Hoji's advisors if not the Lord himself, who watched me impassively, saving any emotion for Otaro.

"Greetings, Lord Hoji."

"Greetings, magistrate, have you returned with my uncle's body?"

"Yes and those of his retainers, they are being tended to now."

"And have you determined who murdered him?"

There was a pause and Lord Hoji's advisors who had adopted a pose of studied indifference to the proceedings, allowed their eyes to drift to where Otaro sat. They leant forward, like ladies at a ball who do not wish to be seen overhearing a conversation but who by the same token will not allow themselves to be kept in the dark.

Otaro paused and breathed out slowly, his voice low and steady, holding his fat little frame erect, his eyes fixed on the Lord.

"It can not yet be determined who launched the attack. I shall have to travel to Lord Ide's domain, of course, to question his men on the subject."

A tension filled the air, the stillness like the calm before a charge; Master Sum regarded me closely, the only one of Lord Hoji's retainers to do so, while the others fixed Otaro with barely concealed looks of contempt.

"You do not think it obvious that Lord Ide is responsible for this outrage? Do you think mere bandits capable of slaying my uncle and six of his trained samurai?"

"No Lord, I do not. Your uncle was a swordsman of great merit and his retainers brave men who fell in the course of their duty.

I would not insult Master Sum, or," he paused, and I could see one of the powdered fellows about to open his mouth "you by suggesting that such men could be cut down by brigands. The attackers were trained samurai, real samurai." He paused here again, allowing the phrase to hang in the air like a challenge and began again before any one could speak. "It is to your uncle's credit that it took twelve such men to overwhelm him and his escort."

"So you admit that the attackers were samurai? Well does it not follow then that Lord Ide is responsible? What other samurai are there?"

"Master Sum," asked Otaro, "it seems unlikely that Lord Ide has a teacher of your skill for his men, but that aside, are his men proficient? What schools do they follow?"

Master Sum's eyes flicked from me to Otaro and he spoke slowly, his voice higher than I expected, but possessed of such authority that it did not seem soft. "They are adequate, but no more. It is not their daily study, they are better counters of rice and bosses of men than they are swordsmen, though there are one or two who show some promise. As to school, they follow the fashions, mostly the Edo schools. They read a great deal and make use of foreign ways, but as swordsmen they are of little account. Brave though. In their way."

This prompted laughter from the younger men, even Lord Hoji suppressing a smile for a moment and then stilling his retainers with a look.

"So twelve of them, could perhaps, take some of our men by surprise and slay them," he said, slapping his knee and rocking slightly. "It is with that in mind that we chastised one of his villages last night and shall do so again, until they face us like men." He watched Otaro now, very closely and the powdered boys ceased tittering.

"Have you applied to the government for a formal feud to be entered into?" asked Otaro levelly. Lord Hoji's answer came, too quickly and too loud.

"It would be unseemly to delay vengeance, for such a heinous act. Do you not think so, magistrate? A samurai's strength lies not in contemplation, but in swift action. To think, equivocate or make excuses could be to make oneself as a woman. Better to strike and have justice."

"Well, Lord Hoji, if you are decided, I shall not trouble you further."

"Of course, Magistrate, I shall not keep you from your duties."

We rose, bowed and took our leave, though as we did so I could not help but notice that the tallest of Lord Hoji's retainers was eyeing me closely. He was a young man, barely out of his teens. Despite his height, his round face combined with the makeup, made him look even younger and rouge on his face, gave it a nauseating sensual cast. As we left, they returned to their conference over the map, Master Sum staying quiet, but the others talking excitedly, at what I realized could only be termed a council of war.

"It is ill advised to go to war without official permission?"

"Very. If it is brief and not too costly, he may get away with it. That is unlikely, though."

"You seem very certain."

"A man who is as hungry for battle as Lord Hoji, is not likely to end a war quickly. It all depends of course. These are interesting times. Your people are making many changes here, Captain Robert."

"How so, what have we to do with this?"

"You were unexpected and we Japanese are not used to unaccustomed things. I, myself, see change as part of life. But some, like that fellow over there, see it as an insult to be avenged."

We had reached the waters edge now and I had stopped whistling. There were small, perfectly smooth stones underfoot and they crunched as one stepped on them. "So what are we to do?" I asked, "The child is still missing and must be found. He was taken, but there was no demand for a ransom."

"That we know of," Otaro corrected, standing by my side. We watched carp, great slowly moving slashes of yellow under the surface of the water, their mouths opening soundlessly.

"You suspect Lord Hoji would keep such news from us?"

"No, he is a good fellow at heart, headstrong, but he would not leave a child in danger. He thinks it seemly to hunt for him because he believes the child to be already dead."

I paused, not looking at him, regarding the pond, its surface dappled by the sunlight through the branches of the willow and stirred by a breeze.

"Do you?"

"One does not scale a cliff face to kill a child, with or without ropes, when one could drop a rock or fire an arrow with equal ease. Also it would be unseemly, men of quality do not lightly do unseemly things."

I did not dispute with Otaro's assumption that skill in fencing was somehow a mark of moral rectitude, but I was glad that he thought the boy was still alive.

"Shall we pay a call upon Lord Ide, if only to make sure that the child is not in his custody?"

"I think we will," said Otaro, "though we shall need horses."

I thanked providence and my creator at this and sent a silent prayer heavenwards that Otaro would succeed in getting us some. He seemed happier now, though the situation seemed as impenetrable as ever. I supposed such crimes as these were more rewarding to investigate than mere disputes over land. Perhaps he thought that there was hope for the boy.

He was more forthcoming and less taciturn. Than he had been in days and I felt around for a topic to keep him convivial. We had passed around the pond, the carp circling with us as we walked. We faced the verandah of the audience chamber now.

The white figure was still standing there, watching us, like a ghost was unaccountably abroad in daytime.

After a pause, I hit upon fencing, always close to Otaro's heart, as the thing to keep his humour gay.

"I notice that Lord Hoji and his retainers carried swords similar to yours." He stiffened and I realised at once that I had blundered. "In that they have the same longer hilt than is usual."

"That is true," he said, "however their blades are made in a deliberately old style, though they are new compared to mine."

Flushing slightly at my faux pas, I thought desperately of some means of changing the subject. I nodded at the white figure who was still regarding us.

"So you think it unlikely that he has ever drawn in battle?"

"Very. In a duel maybe. We are a peaceful people, Captain Robert, as I keep telling you."

"He seems very certain then, that he can kill me."

"He is young and the young are always very certain. Also you are a foreigner and therefore unlikely to have skill with a sword."

I could see the appraising cast in Otaros eyes as he watched to see how his words affected me. When first we met Otaro, having made his living as a fencing master had questioned me at length with regard to western fencing. He was unimpressed with American swords, that much I knew, and I could not blame him. In that sphere at least Japanese mechanics and craftsmen are superior to our own. But as to western swordplay he was unsure, not willing to accept anything less than a test in deadly earnest as proof of its efficacy. Having seen more of the samurai fighting technique then he had of mine, I thought I could acquit myself tolerably well. There were weaknesses to be exploited.

"Look at that young fellow, Captain Robert. Do you see how he stands? See how he carries himself and his swords. That is not a humble fellow. See how they are carried in his girdle, sticking out behind, so that one might knock them without meaning to. He could call that insult and bring you to a duel for it. Yes. He wants to kill you very much."

I studied the young man who, despite his paint, was obviously fit and in training. I reached down and picked up a stone as we walked around the pond again and then stopped, standing not twenty yards away from him now. Our eyes met and I stood there weighing the stone in my hand, seeing his eyes widen as I tossed it in my palm as if I were about to throw it. He shuffled his feet, suddenly unsure of what to do. Disturbed that I might heft a pebble at him. This man who thought to kill me.

I tossed the stone again, caught it, turned and sent it skipping across the surface of the pond.

5

Where I hear a most intriguing tale.

I was writing in my journal when Otaro returned from his conference with the butler and heard that, yes, horses could be got for such august personages as a magistrate and his honoured guest, but it might not be possible until after the funeral of Lord Hoji. Otaro took the implication and we resolved to remain until the funeral was over. Preparations for the ceremony were loud and complex and I held myself in our quarters, writing for the most part. Taking the air in that beautiful garden was no chore and I forgot the circumstances and enjoyed the sunshine.

I had a very pleasant smoke from my dwindling supply of cigars and thought on things. Whoever had the child would kill him or keep him safe and there was little we could do at present to affect his fate, galling though the thought was. The lack of a ransom demand seemed to indicate some other motive than mere greed, though exactly what I could not fathom. Only a journey to Lord Ide's domain, to the other side of the hill as it were, would clarify things. He might be innocent, at least by Otaro's reckoning and I was inclined to trust his judgment. The other matter that required contemplation was my new antagonist, whose name I had discovered was Kaneda. I should perhaps have been more concerned about this fellow, but in truth, ferocious though he appeared, I found it hard to consider a threat of death from a man who wore face powder as a matter of great moment.

I resolved to keep clear of Kaneda, to avoid unnecessary unpleasantness, but I could not allow myself to do so when it might be remarked upon, as that would simply encourage him. I had been marked for death once before on the plains by a brave named Two Shadows and had, through force of character, made him reconsider. It was the difficulty of all civilised men in the wild places of earth, the tightrope trick of maintaining one's dignity as a white man without giving undue offence.

I was brought abruptly from my reverie by the arrival of a menial bearing a message that Master Sum wished to pay a call. I scrambled to my feet and struggled out of my brogans and began searching for my armband. I had no formal clothing suitable for a Japanese mourning, to appear in shirtsleeves would have been disrespectful. But I had fashioned an armband from a page of my journal and I hoped that this effort would be regarded favourably. I had only just regained my composure, after sticking myself rather badly with a pin as I tried to fix my armband to my sleeve, when Master Sum was led in. I bowed low and he returned the courtesy, then looked about, obviously disconcerted.

"Greetings, Master Sum, to what do I owe the honour of your visit?" I asked in my best formal Japanese. He smiled in return and bowed again. "My apologies, Captain Robert, when first we met I was not aware that you spoke our tongue. You are the first outsider that I have met and it did seem unlikely. I did not wish to confuse you. Is your companion here? I came to advise him as to the route to take when visiting Lord Ide."

I struggled to grasp the full meaning of his words, but I noticed that he was considerate, speaking slowly, perhaps as he had heard Otaro addressing me. I fumbled for some courtesy to extend to him until Otaro returned.

"I'm afraid my companion, the magistrate, is attending to some business. May I invite you to stay and perhaps join me in a cigar?"

He seemed confused and I thought perhaps that my meanings was not clear so I offered him a smoke. He stared at it and finally divining what I was about, politely informed me that he had foresworn tobacco until the end of the period of mourning. I realised, that again, I had gaffed and quickly replaced the smoke in my pocket. He saw my embarrassment and kindly suggested a walk in the garden.

As we walked, I took the opportunity to learn more about Lord Hoji, whose death had precipitated this whole series of events. Master Sum spoke slowly, his voice measured as he told me the tale of Lord Hoji and his remarkable swords.

"Lord Hoji was my student, though I am not his retainer. My own Lord died of fever some years ago and I was too old to be of use and was out of favour with my Lord's successor. I was given leave to enter a monastery. But I am old and set in my ways and the life of a monk held no attractions for me. My new master cared little for what I did, so I traveled north to Lord Hoji's domain. I had instructed him as a youth in Edo and he remembered me and gave me leave to live on his lands. I have a small house by a lake in the mountains, given me by his generosity. It is very peaceful there and it gives me time to study my art. Lord Hoji would do me the honour of studying with me on occasion as he had when he was a boy and he was a fine swordsman. Very fine. He reproached himself constantly for not preventing his brother's death and sought to remedy this fault through constant practice. He was my best pupil, though I suppose Otaro would have been his equal, if not his master."

"You really think so? I have heard many tales of my companion's prowess."

He smiled, "Doubtless some are mere stories, but most I suppose are true. Your companion is a samurai of the old style, though he has gained little by it and that, I think, is also to his credit. But this is not germane. Lord Hoji had a vision some years ago, shortly after I arrived in his domain and in the vision, Benkei[9] appeared to him and gave him a pair of swords, the long and the short, the swords he had when he died. Benkei told him that these swords were the work of the smith "Plodding Saburo" and that they would finish the feud between him and Lord Ide. He took them and awoke the next day to find them in his rack.

---

9 A mythological figure, a giant, but good hearted fighter who has some elements of the trickster about him.

He was in a state of high excitement and sent a messenger for me at once.

We examined the sword at length and they were definitely the work of Plodding Saburo, for his mark was upon them. Lord Hoji studied with them even harder than before and from having been a good student, he became a great swordsman. He was convinced that all that was required of him was to practice and be ready, as Benkei had told him so.

"I made drawings of the swords and checked their provenance, proving beyond doubt that they were genuine. In fact while I was in Edo, I consulted with an old sword polisher who was able to identify them for me. They were the last swords Saburo ever made."

He paused and looked at me for a moment, I suppose to see whether I understood the import of what he had said. When he realized that I was both fascinated and clueless, he began again.

"But of course, you do not know the story of Plodding Saburo. It was many generations ago, during a time known as the Time of the Country at war[10], when central government was weak and the great Lords made war upon each other. In that time, in the south, there lived a famous family of sword smiths, who made blades for all the great samurai of the land, the Satsuma, the Higo and the Hizen. All the great families needed their skills. The patriarch

---

10 Otherwise known as the Sengoku ("Warring States") Period, where in the 16th century, local magnates known as Daimyos dominated the Japanese political scene. The magnates struggled against each other in a series of tumultuous wars until they were united by Tokugawa Ieyasu, after his victory at the battle of Sekigahara. This victory allowed him to consolidate his power, assume the title of Shogun and implement the strict regime of social control and isolation that was to dominate Japanese affair for the next several hundred years.

of this family was a smith of superb skill. But to his shame he discovered that his youngest daughter was disobedient to his wishes. She desired to be a smith like her brothers and refused to consider marriage or womanly things until he taught her the secrets of his art. The patriarch had no choice but to consign her to a nunnery, but she ran away and cut her hair. She dressed herself as a man and called herself Saburo and become a village blacksmith. All her life, she studied her art, making pots and pans by day and during the night attempting to make weapons like her father. Most of her attempts were failures, but she made progress slowly though, very slowly, so that the villagers laughed at her and called her "Plodding Saburo". But the years passed and the wars raged and the common soldiers came to her for weapons. And then as her skill increased samurai came too seeking blades. She worked hard and long and after many long years, her work was the envy of the land. Towards the end of her life, she began to work on a pair of swords for a great Lord, when her brother came to her smithy, for her blades with the mark of the bear were the talk of the battlefields. Recognising her at once, even though her hair was short and her arms were thick and brawny, he struck her down from behind, appalled that she could have betrayed her family thus. And so she died, but not before she stamped her epitaph on her last work. She had sacrificed everything, name, family, husband and children, all to craft these two. She called them 'Labour's Reward'."

He paused, watching me intently with quiet eyes as a cloud passed over the sun and I shivered, the macabre nature of the tale unmanning me a little.

"But what is the significance of the name?" I asked. He smiled indulgently, I suppose the tale was a common enough one and would only be told to a child, so I forgave his condescension and pressed him to continue.

"There are tales from the distant past, of smiths who were touched by the gods, who could forge weapons that were not truly meant for mortal men. There are stories of spears that sang death songs for their victims, arrow heads made from the hammered souls of the damned which could pierce any armour and swords that when drawn licked with hungry tongues of flame. I am a simple man, Captain Robert, I believe in what I can see and I have never seen any of these things. But I have seen "Labour's Reward" and I think its magic is a subtler thing than tongues of flame or singing spears. It is the magic of a woman who gave her life for her work. Simply put, it is a fine sword, they are both fine swords – light, well balanced and easy in the hand. But the magic in the blade is such that he who studied with them will be brought further along the way then he could ever travel alone. That is the magic of "Labours Reward". The talent does not matter, only the will, the determination and the work count."

It was a queer tale, this story of blood and smithing, and though the romance of it touched my hear. I could not but let the down-to-earth Yankee in my nature question it.

"And do you believe in the magic, Master Sum?' I said, taking care to winnow any suggestion of skepticism from my tone and watching the old fencing master to see what his leathery countenance could offer up.

"I do not know if I believe in it or not Captain Robert, but I do know that Lord Hoji was a diligent student, but slow and unskilled when I taught him first. It was the same when he became my student a second time. But after", he smiled, "he mastered in a few years things that took me decades to learn. I am a good teacher, Captain Robert. Ask your companion if I am not, but a man would do well to understand his limits. Is that not so? And speaking of your companion, here he comes now."

I looked up and saw Otaro walking through the garden to meet us. He bowed and seemed surprised yet gratified that Master Sum had taken the time to help us on our way. The horses were fine beasts, he added, and we would like as not be held up at least two days by the funeral proceedings. The people were gathering already to pay their respects to their fallen Lord.

6

The queerness of funerals and we are invited to dinner, finally.

The funeral was a strange affair, though I suppose I should have expected nothing less. I discussed the arrangements with Otaro, who assured me that my armband was an elegant sufficiency, but would I please wear my uniform as it would be considered an honour to the deceased. I, of course, agreed.

The castle was awash with people as the six samurai who had been slain protecting their Lord were being buried at the same time and their families were gathering in preparation. I was in our quarters paying some attention to my shako with a brush when Otaro brought me seven envelopes, simple, yet beautiful creations of black and silver paper where Otaro told me I was to deposit a gift of money to the family to help defray the cost of the funeral, and as a mark of respect. His own contributions, jangling with coins, he kept in a small linen bag at his waist.

Counting courtesy greater than economy and aware that I might be cut down by a powdered assassin, I deposited a dollar in each envelope and a five spot for the big chief. Extravagant perhaps, I could hear my father's thrifty Yankee cluck ringing in my ears. Otaro told me that the funeral proper would not begin for another day yet, that there was a viewing or some other business (I am lost as to what the English translation would be) tomorrow, with the funeral the day after. I sighed at the time taken from our search for Lord Hoji's son, but there was more welcome intelligence.

Since the sad news that we had brought with us, the family had been in mourning. Consequently we had taken food in our rooms without formality. Having met Lord Hoji's widow I had no wish to impose upon so delicate and beautiful a creature the unpleasant duty of being sociable at such a time. However, this in no way impinged upon the flush of good feeling I experienced, when Otaro informed me that one of the families whose son had been slain in the attack was holding a formal dinner in the village behind the castle and that we were invited.

The meal itself was in a boarding house hired for the purpose, the family of Toko (the poor dead fellow in question) living some distance away. The meal itself was an epicures delight, as dish after dish of seafood was served, some stewed, some cooked on a small portable griddle or others served entirely raw. The meal was accompanied by sake, their rice whiskey, which was taken warm and sweet. I have never acquired the taste for it. However, my host also plied me with a chilled plum brandy whose exact name I can't remember, but which I found monstrous fine and I must confess, indulged in rather more than I ought.

Otaro and I were seated near out host, a short, corpulent old villain named Hisamatsu whose face bore a long jagged scar, from the last time there had been a rumpus with Lord Ide's men he told us. The whole proceeding was a very jolly affair and similar to the Irish tradition of the wake that I observed amongst our troops in Mexico who were immigrants from that land. I was regarded as something of a curiosity. Even more so when it was discovered that I spoke Japanese, but Otaro was the catch and was pressed into tales of his time in the militia[11] (their sort of police force) and enforcing the law on the open road.

Not everyone could gather around the great man, so some of the company had to make do with me. Most of the talk was boring or over my head, politics mostly, but of the petty kind and wistful remembrances of their last trip to Yedo. I was ignored for the most part. The talk was dull, but there was a certain value in watching the Japanese off their guard, so I thought it best to keep quiet.

Eventually the conversation turned to the murder of Lord Hoji and in particular, the theft of his swords. Their discussions shed no light on the crime. They had no theories that Otaro and I had not considered, but what was interesting were superstitions and tall tales that were trotted out to explain the whole business. Lord Hoji's swords had been made by a fellow called Masurae and were therefore cursed, his death was inevitable. It was to the clan's good fortune that he had left a strong heir. This was dismissed, amid loud boos. What was far more likely, another man said, was that Lord Hoji had been ambushed and killed by

---

[11] I had at first thought that Otaro may have been a member of the Shinsengumi militia, a radical group closely aligned with the Shogunate, who took it upon themselves to police Kyoto. However, there are difficulties with this interpretation; the Shinsengumi were loyal to the Shogun over the Emperor and were in favour of compromise with the West. Also they were only formally established three years after Hood left Japan. It seems to me far more likely that Otaro was involved in one of the other militias or private armies so common in Japan at that time.

Lord Ide using black magic, the only way such a milksop could defeat a man like Hoji. The swords had been taken of course, because they held the souls of Lord Hoji's ancestors. Lord Ide's black magician would torture Lord Hoji's ancestors in the afterlife now that he held their earthly vessel.

I have a tolerance, even a fondness, for the tall tales of barracks and camp. But even I had difficulty hiding my amusement at the parade of spirits, ghosts, assassins, goblins and devious foreign agents who were assigned the blame for Lord Hoji's death. At least, they were blamed until a new speaker found a new culprit and the whole game began again. But the best was yet to come, for another man hiccupped beside me and began seriously.

"If they stop at that, my friends, there is every possibility that Lord Ide, being the low type that he is, consorts with demons and hellish magicians, who can pluck the very soul of a samurai from his sword and force his spirit to do his evil bidding. Who knows, perhaps in the next battle against Lord Ide, we will have to face the shade of our former Lord."

This really was too much and I was only saved from giving mortal offence by laughing out loud, when Otaro arrived to check on me. At the sight of the great man, all talk of ghosts and goblins ceased and soon Otaro was being badgered for the story of the one eyed bandit from Satsuma. Otaro submitted with good grace and told several stories and soon the company was roaring with laughter.

The evening ended most convivially with my host, lolling in Otaro's lap, drunk as an English Lord, while Otaro told the story of how he met the Pope or as he called him, the son of Heaven.

Hisamatsu struggled to his feet to thank the fates that his son had died like a man, his wounds to the front, his sword in his hand and his enemies bodies strewn about him like fallen leaves. His voice choked with emotion, a father's pain at a lost son was evident, but pride too, great pride on his noble, ugly face. He said that in these days not one samurai in a hundred could hope for such a death. Though he added, if the Mikado continued to be the province of milksops and lovers of boys[12] (forgive me, but I report only that which I heard with my own ears) who thought of nothing but their pleasures and giving the country away to foreigners there would be a deal more blood spilt. With that he sat down on his rump with a thud, his sake cup falling from his limp fingers.

He patted my arm in what I supposed was a comforting gesture, though Otaro and I had exchanged glances at the remark about foreigners. Several of the other guests, samurai from the nearby villages, began to clap and laugh too loudly and enthusiastically for it to be anything but nerves. Hisamatsu, his face reddening, clutched at my sleeve. I was unsure of his meaning when his chest heaved and a huge shuddering sob came forth from its very depths. His face contorted and he began to weep. Mashing his head against the blue serge of my uniform coat, his throat ached with inarticulate groans of pain, as he hammered his

---

[12] While Captain Hood's reaction to this comment is understandable, the fact that it was made at all is a little less so, homosexuality being perfectly acceptable under Japanese social mores of the time. Perhaps Hisamatsu simply did not like them.

hands upon the floor. I patted him on the back and told him that he was a proud man and was the father of a son who had died a warrior's death and that he should be happy. That did not seem to abate his grief, but his sobs became quieter after a while and he sniffed and straightened up, blinking tears from his eyes. I to my shame was worried that some mark of his emotion would stain my uniform and that I would have to occupy myself with cleaning it on the morrow, but on closer inspection the damage was not severe and would be the work of only a minute.

Then Otaro made a joke, a coarse one, but the company laughed, even poor old Hisamatsu hiccupped in response and then another was told and soon we were a party again, though we took care not to refill Hisamatsu's sake cup too often. It was as if nothing had occurred and the party continued for some time longer, though we left soon after.

As we walked back to the castle, Otaro leading the way, bearing a neat square paper lantern on a short stick to light our way, something singular struck me, even in my brandy addled state.

"Otaro, remember when old Hisamatsu was speaking of his son, dying with his sword in his hand. It is not literally true, they were all killed while wielding spears. They had no time to draw swords."

"What of it? The old man sees his son's death as he wishes it to be, there is no harm in it."

"But they still had their swords, did they not? These men were samurai, they did not carry common weapons and yet…"

Otaro stopped suddenly and finished my sentence "…only Lord Hoji's swords were taken, the rest were left. That is interesting. I am sometimes very blind, Captain Robert, thank you."

I was brushing off the marks of Hisamatsu's lamenting from my sleeve while Otaro pulled out the mats for bed, when another point struck me.

"That old man was proud of his son, but his grief was very great, but there was no sign of it before the party."

Otaro gave me a quizzical look as he brought a quilt out from a closet

"Some pain is so deep that it may only be shown in front of friends when they are willing not to see it."

"Will he not do so in front of others? What of his wife?"

Otaro rolled over and brought the quilt over himself with a shrug.

"Mothers cry. It is what they are for."

7

*Funerals, some delightful gifts and an embarrassing interruption that speeds us on our way.
I receive too rich a gift.*

The viewing itself was an uncomplicated business. Several rooms in the castle had been set aside for the late Lord Hoji and his retainers. In each room was a group of mourners all dressed in white and a priest who crouched like the original baboon near the deceased and would occasionally issue forth a sonorous dirge from somewhere deep in his stomach, ending in a nasal whine that was most irritating. As was the constant muttering that seems to be the mark of the holy man in the East. One entered, deposited one's envelope with a fellow posted at the door for the purpose and then advanced to view the body, kneeling by the head and moistening the lips of the dear departed with a damp cloth. The poor boys had by this time been subject to the mortician's art and were looking considerably better then when last I had seen them. Yet their reddened lips and white powdered faces reminded me uncomfortably of my shadow Kaneda.

Next, one reached over to a small pot of incense and took a pinch, then tossed it on a burner. This was done three times, so that after you and all your fellows were done pinching and tossing there was a thick fug that made me think of the interior of a Chinese opium den. Then, one rose and made one's way back to the door where a representative of the family would give you a small gift of perhaps a quarter of the value of the money gift you had given.

In this manner, I became the proud owner of one lacquered snuffbox, one set of carved cord toggles in the shape of a dog, a bamboo pipe with a brass bowl and a pouch of tobacco (odious stuff, but a comfort when my cigars ran out), a set of checkers in two small wooden boxes and a little silken sack containing a quantity of rhubarb, which Otaro told me later, with no hint of jest, was vital for the digestive system of westerners.

With such a trove of loot accumulating in my pockets, I had difficulty not assuming an air of levity upon entering the room where Toko, son of Hisamatsu, lay. That put any light hearted thoughts from my mind, as the reason for the old man's grief became all too evident. Hisamatsu's boy had been in fact, exactly that, a boy, of perhaps fifteen years, but certainly not older. His wan expression seemed utterly calm, though I could see some of his bulldog nature in the set of his jaw. His youth was borne home to me as I tossed my incense and moistened his lips, that he had not yet had the samurai tonsure and the dark locks of a boy framed his face, white, almost translucent like the first light of dawn strained through paper.

Two very singular things happened thereafter, one of which was to have a very curious and tragic result. As I returned to the entrance of the room, made my bow and waited to be given my little gift, Hisamatsu was kneeling by the small pile of envelopes, staring fixedly at mine, he seemed rooted to the spot and completely incapable of movement. I smiled at him, my heart touched at the tragedy of a father who outlived his son and touched him lightly on the elbow thanking him politely for his hospitality of the night before and in particular the very special gift of the stories of his son's courage. And with that I took my leave.

The second singular thing occurred when I, following Otaro's lead, came to the larger room set aside for Lord Hoji's laying out. Retainers and courtiers, all in white stood about the room like hung paper lanterns. Lord Hoji's body was at one end on a small dais draped in white fabric. In his right hand he held a fan and his left was on his breast. His body was shrunk, as bodies do in death and the skin contracted so that he still had the bared teeth, that I remembered so clearly from our first meeting on the ledge where he met his end. The morticians art had been most skillfully employed here. Having failed to set the jaw or cover the teeth, the mortician had made his dark brow darker and left his eyes open, so that they glared out at the viewer even in death, so that Lord Hoji appeared like the wood cut ideal of a samurai that he had no doubt been in life.

I tossed my incense and sitting against one of the walls waited for Otaro to do the same when there were sounds of a scuffle outside. There was a banging and the pad-pad-pad of bare feet on wood and then a horrid strangled cry of feminine distress. I glanced about me, surprised and concerned, though everyone was studiously attending to the ceremony. Here and there I could see a jaw tightening, an eyelid flicker or some other sign that something unpleasant that was best ignored was taking place.

Suddenly, there was a high pitched woman's cry of "Devil! Devil! Monster!" and a crash. A great ripping, tearing sound split the air as two servants, a man and a woman, bowled straight through the wall by the body, struggling as they were with a small wild haired woman dressed completely in white. "Devils, devils!" She shrieked and clawed at them, kicking and bucking under their combined weight. Mourners scattered, leaping out of the way, aghast, their mouths open in mute shock. The man on top of her howled and clutched his ear where she bit him, the serving woman was thrown off with a blow, her white kimono splashed red with the free flowing blood of her fellow. The madwoman ran and leaped across the body, staggering as she landed and falling over. "Devils! Ghosts! Demons!" she screamed again, "evil hearted pigs, pigs!" and her voice was a high pitched squeal. Her head whipsawed about, as if searching for enemies, invisible enemies, all about her, when she saw me her eyes widened in fear and shock. Her face was pale, almost completely white, but stained by twin black trails where eyemark had run. Her eyes were livid red like a wound and her teeth, black and shining, were bared, like those of a beast of prey about to pounce. Her whole aspect changed when she saw me however and she quickly backed away. She screamed again, this time in fear I suppose, rather than rage and turned and almost ran into where Lord Hoji was sitting with Master Sum and his advisors, gawped at them, stepped back, stumbled and fell on her rump, backing away as fast as she could manage, her terror evidenced by the trail of yellow liquid she left in her wake. She twisted about, her eyes frantic now and giving sickening sob of utter terror, turned her head skyward and screamed.

"Save us, save us, save him, oh devils, oh dead pig faced devils, oh save him from those devils, save us." The last was uttered in a sad, low mutter of defeat while she gazed down at her hands, bruised and bloody, nails torn from them in the struggle. Then she covered her face and her body shook, silently and without any accompanying sound as the two servants followed by several others grasped her firmly by the shoulders and carried her from the room. A menial stayed to gather up the fallen parts of the wall, collecting shattered pieces of lacquered wood and paper and tucking them under his arm.

Otaro moved to the body, now brilliantly lit by a delicate golden light that speared through the wrecked wall like a shaft of pure gold casting a brilliant yellow glow over Lord Hoji's face. It softened it somehow and he seemed suddenly almost embarrassed or perhaps apologetic, lying as he was in a column of clear light dancing with dust motes and blossom blown in by the breeze.

My friend rose, nodded to me and we returned to our chambers.

"Who was that?" I whispered out of the side of my mouth, glancing about me to make sure we were not being spied upon, any more than usual at least.

"I'm not sure, but I think I might be able to guess." I nodded for him to continue as we reached our quarters.

"That was Lord Hoji's sister in law, the current Lord's mother. Rumour has it she's mad."

Rumour has it? It seemed fairly well informed to me, for once at least.

"She seemed very distressed, by her brother in laws death no doubt, but what was that about saving us?"

"It is likely the ravings of a hysterical woman, which is a pity as she was quite a beauty once, or so I'm told. Her son is devoted to her. The family wanted to put her in a nunnery, but he was obstinate. It's rather sad. Sometimes she doesn't speak for weeks and he has to feed her bean curd with a spoon like a child. Other times, she is not so quiet, which is unfortunate. It will probably delay the funeral."

He sighed and sat down on the verandah and proceeded to pick at his feet.

"Is that likely?" I asked worriedly. "Should we not get on with the search for the boy?"

"True , I don't suppose Lord Hoji will be sorry to see us gone after we witnessed his embarrassment today. I shall make the argument to the butler, that having paid our respects and having pressing duties to attend to, we should be on our way."

Otaro rocked back and forth a little, pausing to study a fragment of skin, when a thought struck me.

"You're not from this part of the country, are you?" He shook his head.

"Then how do you know all this?" I was becoming exasperated at always learning things second hand.

"You know that fellow at the gate, the fat chap with the hare lip?" I said that I remembered him. He was the friendliest of the samurai guarding the walls and would usually greet Otaro with a wave, after checking that he was not observed of course, so as not to break decorum.

"His name's Yamagatu, I went to school with him. He used to beat me severely when I was a lower class man, but he is a good fellow, if a terrible gossip. Always was of course."

This mollified me somewhat and my humour was improved when Otaro finished grooming his feet, gave a contented sigh and rose, declaring that he would discuss the matter of horses with the butler. While he did so I busied myself with my journal and with clearing and reloading my revolver. He returned shortly and we passed several pleasant hours in the bath house, cleansing ourselves and sitting in wonderfully hot tubs of water, soaking. On our return, a servant called to tell us that Lord Hoji understood the urgent nature of Otaro's duties and that horses and tack had been procured for us. We smiled together and I silently thanked that poor mad woman for her unwitting part in sending us on our way.

It is often the habit of Americans, and also Europeans, to denigrate the quality of Japanese horseflesh. This is pure chauvinism. The two steeds presented to us in the stables were as pretty and sweet natured a pair of mares as you could wish for. Certainly, they were small and I resolved at once, that I would walk mine when I could, for I had no desire to give her a sore back if I could help it. They were ponies really by our standards, little more than fifteen hands, but they were solid and doughty and would do us good service on the road. For Americans in particular to denigrate these little horses is nothing but foolishness, as they are the very twin of the Indian ponies found on the plains, where they do great service too. I shudder to think of what would happen if someone tried to force those superb light cavalrymen to do battle on their plains. They would have hot work of it. Those who continue in the folly of making light of the small horse, think a horse must be a titan to carry a charge.

But I digress, they were fine horses, and I called mine Rocinante for she was an enthusiastic and faithful little beast[13].

Otaro seemed less pleased than I with our new companions, but I suppose that is because he was at heart a pedestrian, the Japanese not being a horsey people on the whole. I had returned to our chambers to gather up the last of our things and was thinking of some way of attaching my knapsack to the damnable wooden impediment to horsemanship that the Japanese term a saddle, when I was taken from my reverie by the sound of running behind me.

---

13 Rocinante was also the name of Don Quixote's horse. In the Spanish, which Hood would have known, it translates as "that before was a nag". I can only presume he was making a joke of some sort, the meaning of which is obscure to me.

It was old Hisamatsu, puffed and out of breath and carrying a long cloth bag. He was wheezing and clutching his side, begging our pardon, but he had been told that we had already left. He began then to speak so rapidly that I had to call Otaro to translate for me. I stood there, bereft of any sense of what was going on, while Hisamatsu either excited or upset talked a blue streak. He ended his gabble, just as Otaro arrived, by drawing his charge from the bag and presented me, head bowed, held on his two outstretched hands a samurai sword gleaming with black and red lacquer. He held it there his arms steady as I stood utterly dumbstruck. Otaro gawped openly at the scene and shot me a very strange look, Hisamatsu began speaking again.

"Otaro, what is he saying?" I asked, the old man looked as if he was about to collapse. He was in the throes of some deep emotion.

"He wishes to thank you for your generous gift and your kind words on the occasion of his son's death and wishes to apologize for not being able to give you a suitable gift in return for your generosity at the time and asks that you take this as a token of his gratitude."

I stared unbelieving at the sword, the scabbard shining in the light of day and suddenly realised where I had seen it before. It had been Toko's sword, the one he had died with, undrawn, at his side. Such swords were the lives, nay if some were to be believed the souls of the men who carried them. The idea was ridiculous, but even so. My head swam. I believe I felt slightly faint. What could I have done to deserve this?

My mind came immediately to the dollar I had placed in the envelope as a mourning gift. Perhaps Hisamatsu, having never seen one before and having no understanding of its real value, was at a loss as to what to give me in return? All this was momentary, but I was jerked to sudden alertness when Otaro grasped my arm tightly and put his face close to mine, hissing.

"Take the sword. The gift is offered. Take it."

I stammered that it was impossible, that it was too much and he actually shook me impatiently.

"Whatever his reasons. Take the sword."

I refused again, a hot flush of embarrassment and guilt flowing through me. Hisamatsu's head was bowed and motionless, but his arms, old as they were, were beginning to tremble.

"His wife is dead Captain Robert. His son is dead. He is alone. Do not insult this man. Take the sword. You may never wear it. You are not samurai. But take the sword."

The last was uttered with such vehemence that I believe he would have struck me had I refused a third time. Thankful at least that he had spoken in English and that the old man had been spared the substance of our exchange, I reached out with faltering fingers and lifted the weapon from the old man's hands. He bowed again and gave me a wide smile, which I returned weakly. Otaro clapped me on the back and congratulated me in an overloud and affected manner as I did so. I thanked Hisamatsu in as courteous a manner as I could muster from my limited Japanese and bowed low to him.

Having seen Otaro do the like in conversation with other samurai, I pushed the hilt with my thumb, drawing it out until I had exposed some four inches of gleaming steel. There was a makers mark on the blade that was unintelligible to me, but I complimented Hisamatsu on its beauty and evident sharpness and made a few other compliments whose precise meaning were obscure to me, but which I had heard Otaro pay other sword owners. The old fellow was standing erect now, his hand on his hip, at his own swords. He beamed at me and thanked us both, saying that he did not wish to delay us any more than necessary. We continued to the stables to complete our packing and the saddling and fitting out of the horses. I was still dazed and more than a little shocked by my recent experience and was holding Toko's old sword with one hand, stiffly by my side, almost afraid to touch it. Otaro produced the bag that Hisamatsu had brought it in and tied it up in that, then showed me, rather gruffly I thought, how to carry it on the saddle. We finished our preparations in silence.

Days later when I asked Otaro how he could account for the old man's extraordinary generosity he said that he didn't know, that most likely he had been confused by my mourning gift and embarrassed by his behaviour while we were his guests, particularly his slur against foreigners. His belief in the weakness of the government and his disapproval of its treaties with foreign powers might have been sincerely held, but they certainly should not have been expressed while I was his guest. That was how Otaro saw it anyhow.

Of course, all of this understanding was ahead of me as we left the castle, Otaro taking the lead and I, still somewhat baffled, following on behind. As we made our way down the valley, searching for the turn off in the road that would bring us to Lord Ide's lands, I reflected on the events of the last few days. We had discovered a murder or perhaps an assassination, witnessed the beginning of an undeclared war, investigated a mystery, albeit without much success, and attended several bizarre religious rituals. And yet, outlandish though these events were, they seemed completely in keeping with the land where I found myself. As the castle slowly passed from view and the sun dipped towards it, reddening the sky, my thoughts turned again to Sir Walter Scott and what he would have made of my situation as I journeyed west to avenge a murdered king, find a lost princeling and a magical sword, carrying a sword I could not wear and leaving behind a poor mad damsel locked away behind the paper walls of the dead Lord's tower.

8

A rude awakening.

We travelled along the winding roads for several hours before we reached a gap in the valley which would allow us to turn off and head into Lord Ide's lands. It was a different route to the one we had come before and we made good time, walking the horses for the last two hours to spare their backs. Otaro had returned to his usual taciturn self, speaking little and directing our course with little more than a pointed finger. I was pleased to keep my own society for the time, as I was mulling over the events of the last few days and was happy to be horsed after so long afoot. We made camp at the valley side, where a small spring trickled past a shrine that was some distance back from the road. There was a patch of level ground behind the shrine and it was there that we slept after watering the horses and rubbing them down, a task I took over from Otaro (for in truth he sat astride his mare like a sack of meal and obviously resorting to this method of conveyance by strictest necessity). As I did so Otaro boiled some rice and fish in a kettle which we ate by the light of our little fire. After that we slept.

I woke in the dead of night, the fire now embers, with only the pale light of the moon to guide me. Stars glittered coldly in the night sky above and I rolled over shivering and gathered my blanket about me only to realize that Otaro was nowhere to be seen. I was digesting this, wondering perhaps if he had gone to answer a call of nature and then paused realising that he had done so before we slept. A twig cracked to my left and I froze, every sense straining to discern what was going on about me. I was almost ready to shrug my shoulders and go back to sleep when I saw something glitter in the darkness of the trees. A pale figure, the moonlight casting a wan light over the hem of a perfectly white kimono, stepping silently through the trees. Kaneda, I thought. The swine isn't waiting for the opportunity for a duel, he intends to murder me in my bed. Toko's sword was by my saddle, which I had discarded as useless for a pillow and was some distance away. However, both my revolver and my sabre were close at hand and feigning sleep, I rolled over so that my blanket covered them and I soon brought them to hand. Rolling over again, giving a fair impression, I thought, of a man asleep, onto my back, I peeked through barely closed eyes and resolved to give the would-be murderer as many colt cartridges as I could muster from beneath my blanket. Watching the white figure, I squinted and discerned two more, one on either side of the first. Where was Otaro?

I realized that my first scheme was suicide as the second and third men would simply spear me where I lay. They were no more than thirty yards away and about to step into the clearing in front of the shrine when they stopped. I am ashamed to say

I cursed them soundly, as I doubted my ability to hit a man at such a range in moonlight, but I had no hope as they remained in darkness. That was all rendered moot when suddenly there was a cry and a crash of steel on steel. Two white clad figures dashed out of the treeline swords drawn. I leapt to my feet, heard a yell from Otaro in the darkness and charged. I fired once, missed, the discharge almost blinding me and leaving spots dancing before my eyes. Howling their battle cry, the two came on, their blades a glitter in the moonlight.

I stopped, cocked and fired again and the left most man staggered and jerked back clutching his face. His fellow checked and turned to see Otaro break from the surrounding trees, his face a mask of fury, sword drawn and howling. The man ran uphill. I followed, busting a cap[14] in his fallen friend as I passed and gave chase, Otaro at my side. It was glorious. Combat at its most basic as it had been in the olden days, devoid of tactics or craft, where the general mounted his white horse, someone blew a trumpet and you charged.

Otaro yelled that he would cut him off and dashed to the right as I pushed the pace, wincing as my stockinged feet crushed thorns and briars underfoot. The figure in white, his pale skin flashing as he darted though the pools of moonlight, was only a dozen yards away now. He stopped, turned and bringing his blade up to guard or ready himself for a countercharge, fell behind a tree when I fired again My revolver kicked in my fist and my view was briefly obscured by the puff of black powder

---

14 To bust a cap meaning to shoot. Strange though it may seem to a twenty first century reader, this is an old phrase and refers to the percussion cap which ignited the propellant charge in a musket or revolver.

smoke. I stepped through it, my sabre held out in front of me to guard against a sudden spring from the fallen man, but saw nothing. Otaro appeared, a dozen yards behind the tree where he had fallen and called to me.

"Where is he?"

I motioned to the tree and we advanced on it together, Otaro looking grim his sword held high, his clogs crackling the undergrowth as he walked. I holstered my colt and walked forward, stepping lightly in consideration of my feet. We reached the tree together and there was nothing. I poked the bed of pine needles with the tip of my sabre and felt the tree truck with my hands, half expecting him to appear from the earth like a gnome in a fairytale. We circled back to back and searched for tracks, but there were none leading away from the tree.

Otaro produced a strike a light[15] and lit a fallen bough as a makeshift torch. In the dim light, the bright flame hurt our eyes and the thick clouds of resinous smoke stung the nostrils. After some searching, I found a tree several yards behind where the man had fallen whose bark was split and whose bright yellow heart wood marked the splash of a bullet hole. I had missed.

Otaro smiled wanly and assured me that he had thought I had found my mark, though I suspect he was only being kind. As we searched we talked. Otaro had heard something and spotted the three figures while answering a second call of nature, but by that time, they were between him and our camp. Seeing that they were approaching by stealth, he made up his mind to surprise

---
15 A fire making kit or tinderbox.

them by attacking them from the rear, hopefully bagging at least one and waking me in the process. As it turned out, I had awoken already, roused by some stroke of luck and things had played out as you know. Otaro had bagged his man seconds after the other two had begun their charge and that since then had been trying to catch up. Neither of us had recognized any of the fellows, though they were obviously from the castle. No-one else had cause to be wearing mourning dress.

We walked around, searching for the fellow Otaro had accounted for, but gave it up as an impossible job in the dark. There was at least the chap whom I had felled back at the camp to be gone over. Slowly picking our way through the under growth we made our way back. We were talking quietly, I telling Otaro that I hoped I had not hit the fellow too squarely in the face, as the .44 slug carried enough of a punch to render it unrecognizable. Otaro countered with the suggestion that even so, we would probably find some distinguishing mark upon him, even if the dead man was bereft of his face. We circled for a time and then found the road and worked our way back, my bearings having completely lost in the darkness, when we came upon a very singular sight.

As we passed the shrine, a cloud passed over the moon, shrouding the clearing in inky blackness for a moment (Otaro's torch having long since burned out), we felt our way forward and came upon our camp, where our horses lay sleeping, oblivious to the noise, and the embers of the fire glowed dully in the dark, but there was no trace of the fallen man to be found. Otaro gave me a queer look as I gasped my surprise, drawing his sword and looking about himself warily.

"But I hit him," I complained.

"Are you sure Captain Robert?"

"Definitely, after the other ran, I went past him and put another pill in his stomach for good measure."

"Truly?"

I gave him a rather sharp look at that, "Truly."

I stoked the fire to life while Otaro walked the edge of the clearing, searching for tracks, with more light and aided by a candle I brought from my knapsack we studied the scene, Otaro, his sword sheathed now and his nose close to the earth like a bloodhound.

Two men had entered the clearing at a run, one fell and dropped his sword, the other ran. Otaro gave a grunt of satisfaction, while feeling the earth through the soft bed of pine needles where the man's body had lain. He scrabbled with his fingers, like a surgeon with a tricky piece of cutting and produced a bullet. It was bent and deformed, but it was definitely a leaden slug.. He smiled at me and studied the earth again.

"No blood, Captain, perhaps you missed a second time", he said with a grin that stung my pride. I started to argue, but it was no use, the facts of the matter were clear enough.

"No matter," he laughed, seeing my downcast expression, "he is no longer here to trouble us and is very frightened probably.

We shall sleep and find the scallywag I took in the forest in the morning. I felt him against my blade, there was no mistake."

There was nothing for it but to take the whole thing with good grace. We tossed a coin (a western custom that entertained Otaro immensely) to see who would take the first watch in case the scallywags returned (this was not the first time I found Otaro's choice of English words eccentric or amusing) and, winning I took first watch.

I suppose it is an unworthy thought, but I could not help feeling a little satisfaction at Otaro's chagrin when the next day, we led the horses through the trees to find the spot where he had taken his man. We searched for quite some time before coming upon the trail and Otaro was beside himself with frustration when we reached the end of it.

"I cut him down here," he said forcefully, stabbing the spot with a stick for emphasis and scowling at the trees as if they were somehow responsible.

"They came this way, charged and this one turned as I drew on him, parried my blow like a master, but took the follow through across the belly. I slashed him across the throat to be sure and pursued the other two." He said squatting against a tree.

"And yet, there is no body and no blood". Strange though it was, it was all I could do to keep from laughing at Otaro's aggrieved expression.

"Perhaps his two friends gathered up the body and carried it away, not wanting it to be identified, thus implicating them."

"True," said Otaro grudgingly " but why take the body, his weapon, clear up all the blood, but leave the trail? It makes no sense, none. Why leave the tracks?"

I rattled my brains trying to come up with an explanation that wasn't that they were Japanese and the Japanese do strange, unaccountable, things, when Otaro broke in again.

"He was good, though, very good, to have parried that strike, fast too, tried to catch me a blow even when I had him across the belly, pure Yakamaru school[16]. No fear. Even though he knew he was dead, very good." I tried to break him from this rather morbid musing and suggested that we retrace our steps and try and find the trail of the man that had run. Otaro agreed, but said that we should not tarry too long or half the day would be gone before we began on the road again. We spent some thirty minutes or so combing the ground near where he had fallen and around the camp, in case he had doubled back, but without reward. I had given up with a sigh and motioned to Otaro that we should continue our journey, when he called me over to where I had slept the night before.

He pointed to where I had pushed my saddle away after despairing of it as a pillow. "It seems you have a little friend, Captain Robert, who visits you in the night." I stammered that I didn't know what he was talking about and what did he mean exactly, suspecting that he was making some manner of improper joke. "See" he pointed, brushing leaves and pine needles out of the way and tracing the path with a

---

16 A school of sword fighting popular in Japan at the time, that ignores defense completely in favour of one lethal strike at the enemy. As a result it was popular with some of the more spectacular assassins of the period.

finger "she walked all the way over here, hopped over your saddle and came to your head, stood there a moment, jumped over you and then went on her way. Very unusual that." I leaned closer and saw a trail of paw prints partly obliterated by my fumbling. Exactly the same prints as the ones we had found on the ledge where Lord Hoji had met his end.

"What manner of creature leaves a trail like this?" I asked Otaro, puzzled that a creature could get so close without waking me. Otaro laughed and slapped his thigh, "Captain Robert, it is good for you that you are a brave horse soldier and a gentleman, as you would make no woodsman."

I was about to retort to this jibe, when he interrupted me.

"Those Captain Robert, are the paw prints of a fox."

9

An unlooked for meeting and a sad tale written not in words.

We travelled on for the rest of the day, Otaro seemingly very amused by my puzzlement at the fox tracks. We talked over the events of the previous night and came to the following conclusions.

1. Our attackers had likely been the same men who had slain Lord Hoji, though Otaro was adamant that no-one of the Yakumaru school participated in that attack.

2. The men were likely from the castle as they were dressed in mourning and must have departed at least a little before us to have caught up with two men on horseback.

3. They must have overheard us talking with either Master Sum or each other as otherwise they would have had no idea as to our route. Unless, I pointed out, only three of them were present because the nine surviving attackers of Lord Hoji's retinue had been broken into three groups of three in order to cover several routes.

4. And this was the point I found problematical or at least disturbing. We had obviously come close in some way, however

unknowingly, to the cause or instigator of Lord Hoji's murder or by travelling to Lord Ide's domain we would somehow frustrate the murderers plans. This had to be the case, because if not, why would one waste the skills and endanger the lives of three master swordsmen to put an end to us? I opined that perhaps we had simply drawn their attentions by taking an interest in the incident, but Otaro was not to be dissuaded.

Our discussions had brought us thus far, when we halted to break fast, having some of the eternal rice cakes (one never yearns for beefsteak and mashed potatoes so much as when one is in Japan) and some rather excellent pickled herring when Otaro paused over his bowl and held his hand up. I was quiet and continued my meal, but made sure to loosen my colt in its holster and draw my sabre near me. Otaro rose, stretched ostentatiously and told me that he was going to answer a call of nature. He made towards some bushes off the road, calling to me cheerily in English.

"Some fellow is hiding in the bushes near the horses, go to them, flush him out and I'll catch him." I for my part, smiled and waved in turn and went to the horses. As I near them, I looked around carefully, but saw nothing, then throwing all caution to the wind, I gave a yell as though I stopped someone, drew my pistol and fired. I nearly fell backwards in shock when a swarthy, squat figure erupted from the undergrowth at my feet and ran crying and arms flapping, into the forest. I was stunned and was to my shame, considering shooting the chap in the back, when Otaro leaped from behind a tree, sweeping him from his feet as he did so. I ran to them, to find Otoaro holding the man like grim death as he bucked and wriggled and howled beneath him. A crude, indescribably dirty face, squarish in shape and bearing the tracks of tears down its grimy cheeks presented itself underneath a mass of arms and legs.

"Hush now man, lie still and you will not be harmed," I said in my best Japanese.

He kicked out wildly and caught me such a blow on the shin that I almost dropped my revolver. I tried again, but at this stage Otaro had caught the man by the hair and was punching him solidly in the face. By the third blow, which must have left his ears ringing as he was no slouch, he stopped and was after a few moments sniffing and sobbing quietly through a split lip, but no longer howling. Otaro gave him another blow for good measure and stood up.

"Who are you?" I asked, "and what is your name?"

The man looked at me blankly, not seeming to understand. Otaro brushing himself off held one hand over an other and made a gesture whose meaning eluded me[17], holding his hand, palm down, with his four fingers extended and his thumb tucked into his palm.

"He is a charcoal burner and a tanner, by the smell of him" said Otaro, wiping his hands with some grass and with a look of disgust on his face. The man now shocked from his sobs, was prostrating himself on the ground, bowing frantically and

---
17 I am told that this is a sign used to indicate that the person being referred to is of very low caste, a "four legs" or animal. One that is still prevalent in Japan today. My thanks to Mr. Fintan Hoey for this information.

banging his forehead off the ground, yammering apologies as fast as he was able. He was beyond any reasonable conception of filthy and the stench that emanated from him would have curdled milk. In fact, Otaro told me later, that that was how he first noticed him.

But beyond that he seemed inoffensive enough. I tried to calm him, but my words could have been in Chinese for all the good that they did. He spoke a dialect of heavily accented Japanese that I could make nothing of. Even Otaro had difficulty with it. All that I could make out from his obeisances and cries was that he was glad we were not dead and that he was alive. After much prodding by Otaro, he slowed his talk and began to make sense. He seemed somewhat in awe of me and scared of Otaro, so I asked the questions.

"Who are you?"

"The tanner, Lord. Jengen, the tanner, oh Lord."

"Where is your village? Why are you not with your family?"

I knew that men of his caste[18], like those undertakers I told you of earlier, who deal with certain ritually unclean or taboo professions, dealing with the dead, slaughtering animals and the like, lived together in certain proscribed villagers and were forbidden to stray from them.

"A thousand pardons, my Lord. I ran from there, may the gods pardon me, when the horsemen came, they burned and slew many, they killed my wife and pigs".

---

18 Burakumin, also known as Eta, outcast, or "untouchable," Japanese minority, occupying the lowest level of the traditional Japanese social system.

He began to sob again, Otaro stopped him with a kick and we shared a look.

"How long ago did these horsemen come?"

"Two days, my Lord. I have been running for two days."

So this was how the new Lord Hoji took vengeance on those who wronged him. My respect for the man was fast diminishing.

"And why are you still running, Jingen, why have you not gone back to your village?"

He looked at me, eyes wide with stark terror, his nose running with filth and sputum, and cast about fearfully as if more riders would come charging from the bushes. In a terrified whisper murmured, "The dead my Lord, the dead are abroad and are searching the woods for souls".

I glanced at Otaro, wondering if I'd misunderstood.

"The dead," I asked, "when?"

"Last night my Lord and several nights before that, they move in the trees and take those as they can catch, they are the hungry dead."

The mourners obviously, he had seen them in the forest and thought them ghosts as credulous minds will I suppose, but the talk of them being abroad for many days, worried me.

"Have you seen them, Jingen, these hungry dead?"

"Yes, Lord, in the trees, pure white they are and ravenous too."

"When?"

"These last six or seven nights my Lord, but we kept our doors barred and fires burning and they stayed away, but they came for us after the horsemen."

I asked him again and he said he was sure it had been at least seven days and after much hammering of the forehead on the ground and My Lords and this and that, I began to believe him. This of course complicated matters somewhat. Why would samurai pass this way in mourning almost a full week ago and three full days before the murder of Lord Hoji? Unless of course, they were already planning his death, but even then why don mourning before-hand? I thought we should cast an eye over this village. Jingen could at the act as a guide for us until we reached Lord Ide's castle. Otaro seemed inclined to send him on his way, but I persuaded him to let the fellow, who was now squatting in the shade of a tree drying his eyes and blowing his nose on his sleeve, help us. I offered him some herring and the remainder of my rice, for which he was embarrassingly grateful, though Otaro took on a queasy look when I did so. I found his prejudice somewhat irritating, but I suppose unsurprising, coming as he does from the land of a military despot. The prejudice of the native Japanese against these people is lamentable, but deep rooted, like the attitude of some of my countrymen to the Negro.

While it is written in our constitution that all men are created equal, it is ludicrous to suggest that it is so. However, what is even more ludicrous and deleterious to society is the idea that the superior part must keep the inferior underfoot by legal means such as slavery or by the ridiculous systems of caste.

The white man has nothing to fear from the Negro, unless it be the resentment and righteous anger instilled in him by the lash. Terror at the thought of Negro congressmen and the like is laughable, the Negro will find his niche and be happy and prosperous in his correct place in society. He will be held there by his own natural limitations, those handicaps of his noble, yet childish race. To think otherwise is to show a worrying lack of confidence in one's Anglo-Saxon heritage. It was the sad mirror of our own situation that I saw in Otaro's attitude to the humble Jingen. The enemy is not the humble man, but the cruelty of the system that oppresses him.

Jingen led the way for the rest of the morning as we walked the horses to the village. Otaro, though not grumbling aloud, acquiescing only after Jingen assured us that it lay on the way to Lord Ide's lands. I was unconvinced myself. I supposed the poor chap was too shaken to return to his village alone and thought it better to do it in company. Either way, I wished to see Lord Hoji's handiwork since I had so lately eaten his salt[19].

What we found tore at the heart and forever banished any lingering sense of regard I might have had for the current Lord Hoji, seeing as I did the destructive power of cavalry against a civilian population entirely innocent of wrongdoing. A few rude huts still smouldered here and there, but every where there were bodies, corpses bloated and horrid in the Sun. Jingen ran from hut to hut, weeping and wringing his hand and bemoaning his fate. I read the hoofprints clearly and in this at least I had the better of Otaro. The riders had ridden hard along the road and then a

---

19 An old phrase meaning to have been someone's guest.

scout had been sent forward afoot, his horse being held for him by another. The company, perhaps twenty horsemen altogether, had walked their steeds into the line of trees, mounted and then charged. I saw no sign of preparation of brands and the like, the huts must have caught fire when they were collapsed by the charging beasts. It was a mockery of a cavalry action. They had ridden hard and their horses must have been half blown before they even reached the village, attaining momentum only by the downward incline of the slope. Their dressing was ragged and Otaro pointed out to me signs that they were heard and that the poor inhabitants had run from their homes to bow at the roadside as was the law and custom in these parts.

Jingen was inconsolable, his tears again flowing freely from large brown eyes that rolled in his head as he lay prostrated before a little pile of timber and thatch that had lately been his home. His grief was loud and yammering, a ululating refrain that issued forth in one long howl as he beat his head against the sagging timbers.

"Why? Why? My love, why? Oh my dear ones, why? Why was I not with you, sweetness of my heart, sweet nut of my soul, little ones, why?"

And on and on he went, his lament seemingly untroubled by pause for breath. Even Otaro was moved and could not look on. I leant forward and tried to comfort the man, but he was heedless, lost in pain. I walked about the hut and saw what he could not look upon, his wife, slight and spare of build lying headless by the butchered bodies of her children. Otaro spat suddenly and stepped towards the bodies and I saw that he was trembling. His lip curled and he bared his teeth as he spat again.

"The children were threatened so that the mother would obey. She bent her neck for them."

I said something of Lord Hoji at this point that did him little honour, but Otaro raised a hand and pointed to his feet.

"You blame Lord Hoji unjustly for this. This was the work of our friend the Yakamaru practitioner and his companions."

This I doubted, but Otaro would not be dissuaded, though he granted that whoever had performed such an act was a swine and a monster of the first water. He stole about the village looking for more signs of their passing, I did not join him. The stoicism with which he bore this outrage revolted me a little. My blood was boiling and it took all my self-control to prevent me from crying out and swearing bloody vengeance for these poor people, but it would have been unseemly. Jingen, the poor beggar, was crazed with sadness, unwilling to stray from the wreckage of his house, but unable to face the bodies of his dear ones, so that he would dash in little hopping steps from one point to another as he described a circle around the tragedy.

We stayed there another hour before the horror and the stench of death grew too much even for Otaro. I let Jingen's wailing run its course and then reconciled myself to the situation in the way that my father had taught me to overcome any adversity; through work. I cast about the village until I found a wooden spade and then set to digging a grave. I had removed my jacket and had begun to lose myself in the labour when I realized that it was fruitless. Despite their low station in the world, Jingen's family should be paid all due respect and honour on their way to the next and that meant cremation. Jingen had fallen by one of the shattered houses, his tears run dry, his eyes wide and staring. I tried to rouse him first with words, but sadly found that kicks were necessary. Having selected one of the fallen houses, we began to pile loose wood on top of it until we had a goodly store. Having cooked over an open fire, I knew to take good care to amass more wood than was strictly necessary. Jingen's family would have every dignity we could furnish them with. Barbarous though cremation is, it was better to do it correctly. Done properly our fellow would see his family pass into the air as smoke; done badly we would merely roast them.

Once I had Jingen fixed on gathering wood, I went to my saddle bags and sacrificed another page of my journal for armbands for both of us. I had no incense and substituted what was left of my snuff for the purpose. When it came time to place the bodies on the pyre, Jingen could not do it. I was too weary to strike or even to curse him and so completed the noisome task myself. Otaro looked on, having long since finished his investigations and sat himself oriental fashion by the horses. There may have been concern in his expression, I do not recall. What I do remember was that he waited by the pyre having already lighted a branch with his strike a light, as I carried the last child to the resting place. She was a tiny thing, no more than four perhaps and in one of those strange quirks of fate, death had been much kinder to her than it had the others. She was not bloated and she didn't stink. Her eyes were large and brown, covered by tresses of long dark hair that felt light like the brush of air against my fingers as I closed her eyes one after the other. I was stopped by a soft touch on the shoulder, where Otaro had his hand upon me and I looked up to see Jingen, calm now, his eyes clear with his arms extended. I handed her, soft and light as a doll, to her father who climbed the funeral pyre alone to lay her by her mother and sisters.

10

Beauty then trouble.

We passed a quiet night, oppressed by the melancholy sights of the day and rose in silence. The morning's travel was quiet, Jingen running ahead of us, ducking between the trees and leading the way to Lord Ide's castle. I suppose the surrounding landscape was one of great beauty, I did not notice it at the time as I was peevish and out of sorts and allowed Otaro's poor horsemanship to vex me more than was reasonable.

However, Nature and the blessed hand of Providence eased the burden in a most unexpected way. We were traveling along the valley when Jingen came up suddenly, declaring that we could take a short cut if we wished. I was skeptical and demanded that we should at least stop to water the horses first, to which he replied that there would be plenty of water up ahead. My grumbling at this was soon snuffed out by a low rumbling like far off thunder that grew louder as we moved through the trees, Otaro dismounting only at my insistence, riding as he did without care for his horse's back or for the thickness of the trees. And while nothing so serious as high words had been exchanged over the matter, there was a definite air of mutual irritation as we blundered through the undergrowth, Jingen ahead of us assuring us that all would be well.

And he was as good as his word. After a few minutes of stepping and scrambling up the incline, we broke from the trees, the rumble now a mighty roaring as we stepped blinking into the sunlight to discover ourselves facing a waterfall of breathtaking beauty. It was not great in breadth, but quite narrow, the tremendous roaring that made all talk impossible was accounted for by the height of the fall which could not have been less than forty feet. The enormous volume of fast flowing water shot out clear of the rocks from the height above with surprising force and raised a thin mist into the air. It cooled the surrounding rocks wonderfully and gave a fellow a sudden invigorating jolt sweeping away all rancour and ill feeling. It was even possible to see a bright slash of colour cutting through the mist above, a miniature rainbow arcing across the rushing water. I laughed with the pleasure of it and even Jingen grinned. Poor fellow, he was ever eager to please that morning.

I suggested that we stop a while to water the horses and take our ease. Otaro whom I suppose was still smarting from the sharp way I had spoken to him, agreed and, leaving the horses in my care, slouched into the forest to find that road the Jingen assured us was just beyond the falls. I rejoiced at the unlooked-for solitude, for during my trip I had often found myself isolated from my fellow man by language and education, but I was rarely truly alone. So it was with a light heart that I rid the horses of their noisome saddles and rubbed their legs, checked their feet and fixing them with a halter to free them from the bit for a while and drew cool clean water in a canvas bucket to slake their thirst.

I let them forage as the grass was fine, a deep lush green and of a variety that I was unfamiliar with, but which I learned later provided good roughage with lots of body. My spirits were much lightened by this exercise, as the two mares were charming and took, in the brief rest, a pleasure that was testament to their sweet natures. Rocinante bore watching though, as she balked a little from the fodder I had cut and I thought she might grow colicky if I didn't take care. It was in that supremely pleasant state of mind, cocooned in the soothing roar of the falls, that I brought the mares again to bit. I was resaddling them when I thought I heard something. Leading the horses through the stream at the foot of the falls, I stopped and listened again and this time distinctly heard a shout. Swiftly mounting Rocinante and drawing Otaro's beast behind, I pushed down the road, damning myself for having allowed myself to daydream so.

The road was but a track and swung upwards abruptly, running into the rockface and continuing upwards in the manner of a winding stair, hacked out of the living rock. Faced with this impossible obstacle and suddenly seized with the absolute knowledge that my companions were in trouble, I dismounted and began to lead the horses by the bridle up that narrow and perilous escalade. Otaro's horse shied immediately and would not be moved, Rocinante for her part trembled but still responded and whipping off my neck cloth I bound it around her eyes and coaxed her forward.

It was a tense business and one that tried my nerves more than somewhat. Twice I thought Rocinante was within an ace of bolting and twice she rallied, responding to soothing words as I led her blind up that treacherous path. Though, in truth, it was only a minute or two, it felt like a very age and when we gained the top, which was only two hundred yards from the falls, we were almost directly above them. I was sure that there were rapids behind the trees, I could hear their roaring and see the dancing rainbows in the spray, the colours as clear as a cloudless day.

I heard more shouts now and a shrill cry of terror, piercing a tumult of voices and I spurred on. Rocinante pushing through the low branches, pine boughs whipping across my face. Oh how I regretted my shortness with Otaro now, he could not be expected to know what was best for the horses, my guilt hammered at my heart and I knew that my friend was in grave danger. The boughs parted and I was once again in light, the rapids foaming to my left and ahead of me the stream, narrow, fast flowing and icy cold. Rocinante snorted at the sight and I steadied her, only to start myself when Otoaro, his face crimson, burst from the trees, dragging Jingen after him.

He stood tall now and faced the forest. Jingen moved weakly by his feet, crawling like a blind man or one who has lost his senses. Shouts echoed in the forest as blue clad men emerged from the trees. They were led by a man on horseback, a samurai, a young man who brandished a sword and under his direction, they swiftly fell into a ragged line, thirty or forty of them altogether. They carried rifles, I could not tell the pattern, but they were new and topped with glittering bayonets that shone in the sun and suddenly I didn't think very much of our chances, their thirty against our three.

The samurai screamed at Otaro to surrender, but he merely shook Jingen off and faced them. Their line was greater now, the back ranks filling up with more men advancing through the trees. I began to pick my way across the rocks to cross the river and saw the line shiver back slightly when Otaro stepped forward and realized that these men knew my friend already and did not wish to meet him a second time. The samurai officer howled at his men, his horse prancing sideways out of natural high spirits or because of the excited state of his rider I don't know, and they leveled their rifles. A bayonet clattered on the ground and the samurai screamed again at the trembling man that bent to pick it up and beat at him with the flat of his sword. He seemed to be urging them on and some of them wavered forward a little, but most stayed rooted to the spot. They were afraid of the man with the sword.

The way was clear, they would have great difficulty pursuing us across the river without falling prey to Otaro's sword, one by bloody one. He turned and began to walk, and my heart leapt only to fall sickeningly, as he started to walk along the line, staring at each soldier in turn. A score of rifles followed him and then there was a shot and then another, wild fire, as the men panicked and the whole tearing sheet of smoke and flame blossomed along the line. The breeze caught the smoke and it billowed along the river, white and choking as Otaro stepped out of it and drew his sword. The fire had been high.

And then I knew of course, I realized that he could not run from these men, his samurai code forbade it and that he would stand and die rather than breach it. For myself, there was nothing else for it, and cursing Otaro for a chivalrous idiot, I shortened stirrup and loosened my sabre as soon as I reached the other side of the chill water. I had gone unnoticed, so hypnotized were the men in blue by Otaro's defiance. I spurred Rocinante to the trot and as I drew my sabre, heard shouting, hoarse and panicky, through the powder smoke. As I saw the samurai officer, a youngish man, through the clearing smoke, which was very thick for a single volley, I raised my sabre and felt the earth tremble as Rocinante quickened beneath me. I gasped great lung fulls of air and laughed at his horror and surprise when he saw me in his turn, his flat yellow face contorted in astonishment and losing control of his beast so that she pranced sideways again, which almost cost him his seat. I spurred on and breathed deep the acrid tang of powder filling my lungs and I huzzahed as Rocinante and I plunged through the fug. There were shots to my left and I heard screams and a long ululating howl that chilled me even as I realized that Jingen must still be alive. Rocinante crashed sideways into a rank of men and then sprang forward so quickly that I barely had time to backhand a screaming fellow across the face before we were on again. I rose in my stirrups, soldiers now crushed around me, bringing my sabre down to my right and left, cutting all around me like a maniac. Rifles banged to my right and I speared one, who, braver than his comrades, had tried to present his piece to my chest. Another banged and I feared Rocinante was hit as she leapt forward with a will, trampling men in her path and carrying me through the line into the struggling mass of panic in the trees beyond.

Men blackened, burned and blinded by their own powder (which produced an inordinate amount of smoke, I noticed it even then), were running and I caught the hysteria in the air. Otaro and Jingen were out there somewhere, I needed but to come around. Otaro might turn up his nose at retreat, but he could not disdain rescue surely? Or perhaps Jingen at least I could save. I whirled about, Rocinante whinnying wildly and made for where I thought them to be. A Minie ball[20] plucked at my sleeve and I hallooed again, riding down a screaming Japanese in the confusion. I felt the unholy exhultation of the charge, a sudden dizzying release, as I beat about me with my sabre, smashing raised guns and bayonets aside and slicing arms, faces and heads to bloody ruin. Here was the true nature of man, each breath a cry of victory, guiltless, terrible and innocent of all restraint. In the charge one lives for a moment as a savage, free of conscience and with all trace of Christian civilization stripped away, completely free, but terribly so.

---

20 A cylindrical bullet as distinct from a musket ball. At the time of writing, they were the latest thing. In the United States any bullet fired from a rifle musket was called a Minie ball."

I saw Otaro for a moment through the crush of smoke and running men, on one knee while three soldiers tried to pin him with bayonets. My friend moved swiftly, cutting slivers off their rifle stocks as they jabbed at him and calmly slicing away the fingers of the first man that had tried to skewer him. Jingen was rolling on the ground with another, struggling and they tumbled together into the shallows of the stream.

As Otaro's first opponent turned away, clutching at his maimed hand, my friend regained his feet and began to pursue his other two attackers, whose panicked yelps and pallid faces told that they wanted no more of it. He had killed one and was about to fell the other when the bullet came. I did not see who fired it, but only gaped as he lurched to one side, his hand at his breast. The fellow that had been backing away from him now pressed forward ready to give him the bayonet, but forwent the pleasure when he saw me making for him. There was another disjointed volley and I was on the ground.

I have spoken with men who have suffered near mortal wounds and they have often described a strange sensation akin almost to drunkenness overwhelming them at the moment of wounding. All I felt was a burning pain in my lungs and a profound nausea, followed by a ringing in my ears. I suppose, if I wondered at all, I wondered what was wrong.

11

*I am condemned to death, and then resurrected.
Also a strange meeting.*

First there was darkness, then an agony in my chest and belly. I gasped and the motion brought a tang of pain to my mouth. I lay on a bed, barely capable, each breath a torment and cast my eyes about as the darkness seemed to fade somewhat. There were beams above me, a bolster beneath my head and a thick cover over me. The weight of the cover on my chest was a torture and I weakly tried to push it off. Bile rose in my throat and I became dizzy and fell into sleep.

I dreamed strange dreams, of my mother reading to me as a child when I was with fever. It was late and she wore a night gown and a few of her russet curls escaped from under her night cap. She rocked in her chair and read me "Eloise and Abelard", one of her favourites which I didn't think much of. Her voice was a balm to me though, she would never let Mami read to me when I was sick, but always did it herself. Her face in the candlelight was beautiful, a soft golden glow delineating her strong chin and clear honest features. She turned the page.

I dreamt of Otaro falling beneath the second volley, his back spattered with bullets and falling, falling amongst Jingen's children in the fire. My head ached and my throat was dry, pain mixed with sickness in my mouth as my head was moved, pushed and held.

I held a revolver in my hands, a French pattern, not my own Walker. I turned the key and released the cylinder, removing the caps from the nipples as I did so. I drew the cartridges and opened the traveling case of rich wood where I kept my oil and rags. I cleaned and reassembled it, surprised that my hands found the work so familiar. I thumbed the hammer and put the pistol to my ear, turning the cylinder with my palm. The mechanism clicked smoothly. There was a sweet smell of horseflesh in the air and my head ached. This must be a dream I thought, I've never had a pistol like this. I wonder if it is really assembled like this?

I woke or thought I woke and felt a presence in the room, a woman, I think. She had that scent about her. She pulled at the blanket and I sobbed aloud. A small soft hand restrained me and my head swam. Her fingers were cold and I tried to turn away, only to suffer the indignity of having my chin firmly held and a warm salty broth spooned into my mouth as if I was a babe. I could only manage a few mouthfuls, spluttering even through those. At that she seemed to grow impatient and left.

I felt my chest in the darkness and winced at the threads of pain writ across it, the wetness beneath my fingers told the worst. A musket shot to the trunk was invariably fatal, though rarely quick. I thought with horror of my friend Dragoon Hooper shot from the saddle at Beaune Vista. The poor fellow had lingered for a week, suffering fever and then madness before death claimed him.

My descent into this slough of despond was only hastened when the memory of my friends death came back to me, the wound still fresh in my mind. I ached at the memory of him falling beneath the bullets only to be pinned by the bayonets of those vermin. I wept tears of shame at my selfishness, only remembering him now, my pain wracked chest heaving as I recalled the piteous business. Though he was a pagan, he was as an honourable and noble a heart and as constant a comrade as one could have wished for.

I thought of him stretched lifeless on the field and cudgeled my brain to think of an appropriate prayer, feeling all too clearly the neglect I had allowed to reign in my spiritual affairs. How long had it been since I had prayed? It was a far cry from my days in Mexico or Italy when I had made a point of it, spurred by the simple fact of being surrounded by the Romish faith at every turn. How I lamented my laxness now, now that I was to die alone, without benefit of priest or friend.

I resolved to put this right as best I could though the time was short. I thought long on my sins, sins of wrath, sins of pride and intemperance, my fatal weaknesses of character in Yokohama and the girls with whom I had spent time there. These weaknesses in particular would have pained my mother, who had often despaired of my ever taking a wife, but would have died of shame if she had known that I trucked with whores. I thought of the lives that I had taken in battle, could some of them have been spared? I knew that murder was unconscionable, but that life taken in heat of battle was no sin. But had all these been fair fights and necessary? I had always counted Gideon and Joshua amongst my guides in this respect, but could I be sure? Innocent blood does not easily wash off. My disdain for the Papist faith has always come from their treatment of confession as something to be administered by a mere priest and not by God himself. Their gimcrack absolution smacked of the fairground barker and the snake oil peddler to me.

The sweetness of prayer lifted my heart somewhat and God pardon me, I said a prayer for my lost friend, pagan though he was, I'm sure he would have been washed in the blood of the lamb if he could. It was with such thoughts in my head that I fell again into a deep sleep, this time thankfully bereft of dreams.

I was awoken by a bright light and a sensation of being carried. I thought for a brief moment that I was about to meet my maker and resolved to do so as one should. I had begun the Lord's prayer when a sudden stab of pain made me cry out and I was overwhelmed by a sudden choking odour of tobacco.

"Sweet Jesus, you're not a Methodist, are you?"

My eyes sprung open and despite the pain, I gasped in astonishment to see at the red, heavily mutton chopped face thrust up again my own. It was a florid face, forceful with a strong chin, the teeth stained with tobacco were set in a wide grin and also held a briar pipe firmly between them. Large, curiously liquid gray eyes sat at either side of a boxer's nose and they shone in the blinding sunlight, only reinforcing the impression of ferocious pugnacity put forth by the bright red whiskers and the mass of unruly hair that completely surrounded the face, like the comb of a fighting cock.

I was engulfed in a cloud of pipe smoke that set me coughing, so badly that tears sprang to my eyes at the pain in my chest and my recent resolution to piety sadly not withstanding I roundly cursed the man in the foulest of terms. He laughed and clapped me on the shoulder, which brought more curses.

"Well, no Methody you Sir, with such language, by God," he laughed and slapped his thigh, "and I for one am thankful for it. You'd be dull company".

He stepped back and looked me up and down and I took the time to do the same to him. He was a short man, though he held himself erect to make the most of what he had. The impression was exaggerated by the immense depth of his chest. He had the trunk of a Titan and the sleeves of his red coat bulged with muscle. His large head sat on a pair of shoulders that could have easily done the work of a team. Beside his red coat, which was of a military cut, though it lacked facings and insignia, he was shod in boots of gleaming black patent that would have put my brogans to shame and wore black trousers that were tight about his short, thick legs.

I was lying on a mat in a room whose sliding doors had been pushed back so that the place was full of sunlight. I raised my head to see that it faced out onto a gravel-filled courtyard studded with rocks of various sizes, but with no discernable order to their arrangement. My companion smiled broadly as I stared blinking around me.

"I suppose it is time for introductions, as it is unfair of me to hold you at a disadvantage any longer, Sir. I am Major Fitzpatrick, late of the army of her Britannic Majesty, Queen Victoria. Your servant, Sir", he said with a bow.

I goggled at this for a moment before remembering my manners.

"I am Captain Robert Hood, late of the 2nd Dragoons of the army of the United American States. Your servant also, Sir. You'll forgive me if I do not rise". It was poor stuff and came out awkwardly, but it was all I could think of at the time.

"Not at all, dear boy, not at all," he said with a wave of the hand "you've had a nasty ding about the head and chest, take your ease, rest up and then we'll talk like gentlemen."

I was much confused, was this Major Fitzpatrick an idiot? Did he not know that my wounds were mortal? Or was he simply trying to be kind? I struggled to remain calm and I was suddenly surprised not to find myself more gratified at meeting another white man, but to find him an irritation.

"You'll forgive me Sir, if I do not share your optimism, I have seen some campaigning and in my experience wounds such as mine are invariably fatal. But I thank you for your kindness".

He regarded me very oddly at this and shifted his pipe in his mouth, furrowing his brow. "Fatal, old boy, whatever do you mean? It didn't even break the skin." This was too much and my cheeks burned with strong emotion as I tried to find words to speak.

"You were shot four times, old chap, but they never broke the skin." He knelt over me and poked me in the chest so hard that I found it almost impossible not to whimper like a cur. "Bruised badly of course and then there was that nasty one to your head that did the damage, but even at that your thick Yankee skill saved you from any trouble there." He found this very funny and broke into a "haw, haw, haw", a short barking laugh, that rattled his pipe in his teeth and made his whole body convulse with merriment.

I was about to give vent to a violent outburst, but I fought it down and changed the subject. "Where am I then?" I asked in as level a tone as I could manage.

"Lord Ide's castle, the boys picked you up and carried you back after the scrap by the falls. Some of them wanted to kill you of course. By God you cut them something cruel for just two men, but Nobunga at least had the wit to realize that I would want a word with you." He finished this by drawing deeply on his pipe and searching his pockets for something, finally drawing out a shiny new paper cartridge.

"Here," he said, tossing it to me and to my surprise (and some pain) I caught it, "there you have the root of the matter". I must have looked perplexed. "Bite," he said and I did mechanically, the instinct for loading a musket not having left even in my parlous state. My face must have betrayed my confusion for he laughed his "haw, haw, haw" again. The salty bite of gunpowder was not there, there was a touch of it alright, but the cartridge was for the most part like dry ash.

"No bloody use, is it? Turns out the swine who makes Ittei's cartridges has been stinting on the saltpeter and flogging it to the damned farmers to line his own pockets. Happens all the time of course, but he must have miscalculated with this batch though, as the balls barely cleared the bloody barrels. Of course most of the time they're not shooting at anything so no-one notices." He finished this with his strange little affected laugh again and slapped his thigh, his head bobbing back and forth as he did so.

"Might as well have been loading them with bloody charcoal, for all the good they did, surprised myself really, that enough of them went off to put you down. Of course, at close range." he made to poke me again but despite the discomfort I brought my hand up in time to dissuade him, "they'll knock you about a bit, hence those rather nasty bruises on your belly and the mark on your head. Lucky that one really, probably would have killed you if it had hit straight on, rather than creased the back. But still, it's a rare man that can say he's been shot three times in the belly and once in the noggin and lived to tell the tale, what?"

As it can be imagined, my spirits took flight at this intelligence. I was delivered. I laughed in relief and the Major joined me, his face growing redder and redder. That room was so suffused with merriment that any normal man joining us would have thought us both hysterical or think that he'd arrived in the aftermath of a particularly good joke. My thoughts immediately turned to Otaro and I asked Major Fitzpatrick for news of him as he sought to regain his composure. Wiping tears from his eyes, he waved the question aside. "He's being taken care of, old chap, never fear, he wasn't badly cut up at all, but the crux of the matter is, not to put too fine a point on it, and notwithstanding that it is damned fine to see another white man, what the hell are you doing here?"

In my heightened state, please remember that I had just found myself delivered from an expected agonizing and ignominious end, it did not even cross my mind to ask the same of him, but I launched into a description of my adventure of the last few months. I told him of my time in Yokohama, my meeting with Otaro, the mission my father and his investors had entrusted me with and our adventures up until we had been ambushed by the waterfall. I ventured to suppose that we had been mistaken for Lord Hoji's men and after such signs of their passing as we had seen, it was understandable that Lord Ide's men would be disinclined to parley with those they saw as trespassers.

"So you see," I said, "it's all been a terrible mistake. My friend and I were guests of Lord Hoji and came here in the hope of clearing the whole matter up." Major Fitzpatrick listened to my tale with every sign of attention, seating himself in the Japanese fashion, which caused the trousers about his thighs to creak alarmingly, and puffed on his pipe pensively so that he was constantly garlanded by a wispy wreath of smoke.

"So your friend, the Japanese chap, is some manner of sheriff naobob from Yeddo. By Jove, I don't doubt, they'll not be best pleased when they find out he's been knocked about a bit, pity." He sucked on his pipe and turned his head to the rafters, exhaling a long plume of smoke. "Well, I can put you right on one matter anyhow. It was none of these gentry hereabouts that did for your Lord Hoji, none of them are worth a damn anyway, too busy stealing my bloody saltpeter for one thing. They're blood-thirsty enough. The evil little bastards are drawing lots to see who gets to behead poor old Yoshi, damn his eyes. But assailing a chap as handy as you say this Lord Hoji fellow was would not be their game at all by my understanding. That and Lord Ide does not have so many samurai about the place, that half a dozen of them could leave without it being remarked upon, you have my word on that."

This frank denial seemed genuine enough, slightly scornful even, but if not Lord Ide's men than who?

"Well, in that you seem to be in complete agreement with my friend Otaro. He also thought it was most unlikely. Though I suppose it's gone beyond that now the new Lord Hoji has taken the law into his own hands."

"Absolutely right, old boy, there are few things as tiresome or destructive as a young fool with a grievance and a title". A sentiment I was much taken aback by, though as I agreed with it myself, supposing that an Englishman would naturally support the ancient rights of the aristocracy. I do not know whether it was this or the unaccustomed company and my weakened state that caused Major Fitpatrick to declare our interview at an end. He rose and, urging me to take my ease and husband my strength, said that he would call on me that evening. I was still unsure of the time, due to the blow I had received to the head, but I supposed it was late morning. And that I was forced to do after he left, as both my clothing and my effects had been taken from me and I did not wish to venture out clad only in the dressing gown in which I slept. I dozed most of the day, gathering my strength and formulating those questions that seemed to me most pertinent. They were as follows.

1. If my appearance at the castle required explanation, so did Major Fitzpatrick's. Foreigners were banned from the interior of the island on pain of death without exception. Only Otaro's august connections and anomalous rank amongst the Nipponese made my presence possible. What was Major Fitzpatrick's excuse?

2. If Lord Ide had nothing to do with Lord Hoji's death, who did?

3. Now that the new Lord Hoji had made his hostility clear, what did Lord Ide intend to do about it?

4. Where was my friend being held and to what extent has he been "knocked about a bit"?

I rejoiced at the news that Otaro was still alive and congratulated myself on not disclosing the fact that Jingen had been with us. Fitzpatrick had made no mention of him, he had in fact specifically mentioned "two men", so I sent an earnest prayer heavenwards that Jingen had escaped in the confusion and that the poor fellow was out of this mess. If he had, it was well for him. Even after learning of our pacific intentions I doubted that Lord Ide would have been over-fond of the peasant who had left his allotted village to lead two strangers through his lands. As always happens when the affairs of Lords and princes and high men of state are at risk, the ordinary fellow is likely to be trampled underfoot. I had been pondering these and other matters when I was shaken from my rest by a horrid shriek, so piercing that it chilled the blood and brought me to my feet and searching for a weapon despite my injuries. I was obviously under surveillance, for as soon as I had roused myself I was confronted by a servant girl who urged me to return to my bed. "It is nothing, it is nothing", she repeated when I wordlessly indicated the reason for my disquiet. Then, overwhelming me with a rush of Japanese that was beyond my comprehension other than that I should lie back and be a good gentleman, she bundled me back into bed.

This noise, coupled with the memory injurious to my vanity, put me in no good humour. I examined my dressings, to discover that my chest had been bound, probably against the danger of a cracked or broken rib and that the dressing had been coated with a clear unguent that had suggested blood to my touch the night before. My head was similarly bound and only on my stomach could I see the livid and bloody bruises that decorated my flesh. I was attempting to console myself as to my luck, when Major Fitzpatrick returned somewhat flushed and inquired after my health. I gave him that it was as well as could be expected, but what most concerned me was the awful racket that had interrupted the otherwise peaceful course of the day.

"That was poor Yoshi getting his comeuppance. He was the chap who stole the saltpeter or at least the one that was blamed. They finally got around to beheading him, pour encourager les autres, no doubt, but they botched it of course. Took three blows in the end, poor devil."

The news sent a shiver down my spine, reminding me once more of the half-barbarian land that I found myself in. The very thought of how a beheading could go wrong was chilling, and momentarily distracted me from my plan of questioning the Major in depth, so I found myself quite outflanked when he began to speak of common-place things.

"Suki told me you were restive so I supposed I should come down and see you, though I had been meaning to do so as soon my duties allowed. Tell me, you don't know that awful fellow Harris do you?" He spoke of Mr. Townsend Harris[21], the American consul in Japan, whom I had met, much to my regret,

---

21 Harris, Townsend (1804-1878) - U.S. politician and diplomat, the first Western consul to reside in Japan, whose influence helped shape the future course of Japanese-Western relations.

and I could not help but agree with Major Fitzpatrick and most of the international settlement would have been with us. That the man was a self-important oaf.[22] We spoke of him and other folk around Japan that we knew in common. There are so few foreigners in the country that everybody knows the others business and it really is like a village.

The Major had brought a jar of rice wine and we soon became quite companionable. He became quite vociferous on the subject of the money-changing monopoly, which is a great evil, being as it is merely an officially recognized system of graft. It corrupts those Japanese and foreigners that have any contact with it, which is simply everyone. He was also scathing about the character of the Japanese themselves; their heightened sense of amour propre, their insistence on their own ludicrous superiority in the face of all evidence, and their overweening self-regard. In this he singled out the nobility as the worst offenders, "Mark my words, Hood. If anyone makes anything of these bastards, it'll be because they organize the merchants and peasants, venal little swine that they are. But at least they know how to get ahead, unlike the gay blades of Yeddo."

I am a very dull fellow and the subtleties of parlour conversation and intrigues of any sort are beyond me. But I did realize this at least. Major Fitzpatrick had no reason to be in Lord Ide's castle. No reason that was consonant with propriety at least. But I could think of one reason that he might be present in a place

---

[22] In fact he was so unpopular that certain Americans living in Japan did not celebrate Thanksgiving simply because he encouraged them to do so. The merchant and journalist Francis Hall wrote that "Mr. H is so unpopular with his countrymen abroad... that they are not at all willing to please him in this matter." The Journal of Francis Hall 1859-1866.

where by law foreigners were to be beheaded. He was present as a drill instructor, which would account for the drill of the men who had faced us at the waterfall, which had not been bad. The Major might also have been the source of the muskets they had been carrying. The cartridge he had shown me had been for a musket of the very latest type, probably an Enfield which was similar in many ways (and in truth probably superior) to our own Springfield. Supplying the men with ammunition from England would of course be a problem, which is why they had been making their own cartridges, the small greased paper packets that had lately caused them so much trouble elsewhere in Asia[23].

All this came to me in a moment and I became very much more wary of Major Fitzpatrick, who was obviously playing some sort of deep game. That said, he was becoming somewhat red in the face, and loudly lamenting the lack of anything approximating claret, decent or otherwise, on this whole "damned island". I thought it best to let him continue, as his tongue was doing plenty of wagging all by itself. It soon became obvious that the man was lonely and simply wanted company. So, as the night wore on he became more and more talkative. I learned, refilling his glass as often as my weakened state would allow, that he was Major Edmund Patrick Michael Fitzpatrick late of the 88th regiment of foot and that he was the second son of Irish landed gentry in somewhere called Cavan. He had served in the Crimea which impressed me, as I had heard that it had been a

---

[23] Captain Hood is probably referring to the Indian or Sepoy Mutiny of 1857, which was allegedly sparked by a dispute over new cartridges sealed with pig and cow fat, both of which would be spiritually taboo for the Hindu sepoys.

frightful campaign, where he had made his majority, but he'd had little advancement since then. There was a title of a sort. His father was a Lord, but also a gambler and a drinker and as a consequence there was little of the money so vital to preferment in the British army. Which is why he found himself here, where he hated the food, hated the climate and thought the beebees[24] (what-ever they were) weren't up to much either.

I pressed him a little on the subject of his duties, which he had already spoken about in disgruntled tones, at which he stopped and gave me a sly smile. So much so that I thought I had pressed him too far, when he laughed and exclaimed, "Why lad, to turn this rabble into soldiers, for they're needed and with fellows like that Lord Hoji gentry you're so fond of, they're sore needed indeed. He's a bastard. It's like this, old boy, very simple really, all these Lords are pretty browned off at being ordered around by this Bakafoo[25] of theirs, none of the bastards are worth a damn anyway. They all claim to be soldiers, but they're damn box wallahs[26] the lot of them. But even a greedy little box wallah can see which way the wind is blowing and it's not blowing very well for the Shogun and his gang, your Commodore, Admiral, whatever you're having yourself, Perry did for that. Put the shits right up any Jap with enough sense to realize that steam and guns beats swords and hoighty toighty manners and drinking bloody tea all day. So the smart ones, like Lord Ide, not that you'd think

---

24 I can only guess, but I think what the Major may have said was "Bibi", a corruption of the Hindi word for girl common in British army parlance of the time as a term for prostitute or camp follower.

25 Literally meaning Tent government. The ruling administration of Japan during this period.

26 Box wallah, a pejorative term for an administrator or civil servant.

it to look at him, ugly beggar that he is, are making nice with the fellows that can sell them the good stuff. You mark my words, boyo, there's going to be something of a bloody parliamentary reshuffle in the offing and it's not going to be done with pens and that's for sure."

As he became drunker and drunker, his voice changed and the strange drawling accent had affected at our first meeting with it's slurred R's and W's and its "haw-haws" had become something broader and more recognizably Irish. I had supposed that all the Lords and such in Ireland were English, which is why the rest of the priest-ridden country were so anxious to leave and plague us with their drinking, fighting ways. But as the night wore on it, it became more and more apparent that this man that I had taken for a redcoated Englishman had more of the Bowery thug in him that I had thought. I turned to flattery.

"You've done a fine job, Major, the fellows didn't run, even when charged in the flank."

"And," he banged his cup for emphasis "while their powder was half bloody useless and they had to beat that chap with the sword half to death to take him, when they should have just killed him. Would have been less bother. Bastards."

My heart was in my mouth and I quickly changed the subject, asking how badly Otaro was hurt might tip my hand, "So are they done, Major? Have you passed them out? When will you be back with your regiment?"

This gave him pause and it was with a nostalgic look that he repeated the word "Regiment, the good old Rangers! I've been away too long, the lads will have all changed. I'm detached, you see".

He squinted and tapped the side of his blunted nose with a thick sausage of a finger. "Indefinitely, detached, posted with no posting at all. Not even here, really. I say Roberts, Hood? Robin Hood?" He laughed at his own joke, "shouldn't have said that about your friend, that he was a bastard I mean. Sorry about that old boy, but he's made things damned complicated. He's brave alright, took five of our lads with him and he's handy with that sword of his, unlike half the arse bandits around here, but d-d-d-deuced, d-d-damned, deuced difficult thing you see because of who, whom? He is and who he knows! Cheeky little yellow brave monkey. No, not monkey! Gentleman." He added with the solemnity of a drunkard.

You can imagine my consternation at the Major's words. Here were high matters of state and intrigue far beyond my understanding or capacity to unravel. I cursed that I had not Otaro's brains for such things and in the same moment became aware, that "difficult" was a very dangerous word and that far from being delivered as the victims of some terrible mistake, we were in fact prisoners. The Major rambled on some more until he dropped into slumber, swearing fitfully as he sat legs stretched out against the wall. Rising with difficulty, I made my way to the door, to see what possibilities for escape there might be, when I almost walked into the young woman who had tended me. She, whom, I had learned, was called Suki, and another servant of the house bore the Major away with such ease that I realized that this was a regular occupation for them.

As is turned out, the house that I was in was part of a larger fortified manor, and as soon as I put my head outside the door I was met with the solemn stares of two guards holding Enfields posted by the far side of the graveled courtyard, which was the usual assemblage of paper walls and wooden beam work. I cursed my luck and my injuries which, though comparatively light, became more difficult the more I moved about. Suki returned to collect the empty jars and cups and motioned to me that I should rest. I nodded, hoping that I could at least conceal my knowledge of Japanese, which might serve me as a trump card.

How much better would it not have been, if we had simply pursued the land case that had been his original charge and avoided the morass of swordsmen, murder, kidnapping and politics, domestic and international, in which we found ourselves. And it was with these craven and unhappy thoughts that I fell into a fitful and anxious sleep.

12

A marvelous breakfast.
I meet a company of gallant hats and I am imprisoned by them.

The morning began with soup, or at least a sort of fish broth, that Suki insisted on spooning into my mouth even though I made it clear that I was more than capable myself. Suki was of the opinion, shared by women the world over, it would seem, (my mother would have agreed with her), that in times of sickness soup was the only thing. And so soup I must have. She really was a quite exceptionally pretty girl and she had the shape of a woman, which so many Japanese women lack, but she brought with it an air of companionability and good sense, that had nothing to do with conversation. Her solicitude while I was with her was never less than total and though I only spoke to her in my own tongue, she never failed to address me correctly, though to her understanding I would have never known the difference. It is a small thing, but she was a ray of sunshine in an otherwise dark place and it would not do to forget her. When she had finished with me and I had walked about a bit as I had some necessities to attend to, I began to realize that her poultices were having a marvelous effect and that my bruises which were as bad as any I have ever had, were fading noticeably. The guards, though they took a definite interest in me, did not bestir themselves if I sat quietly so I opened the sliding doors and looked out at the courtyard which was deserted and not a patch on the gardens of Lord Hoji's castle, but at least it allowed me air and sunshine and gave me space in which to consider our position.

We were prisoners, that was clear. We had stumbled upon something that was of great moment to the Japanese court; a local Lord assembling a force of men drilled in a European fashion and armed with imported firearms supplied by foreigners. Perhaps, even by the British government itself! All European powers were attempting to curry favour in Yeddo at the moment. What if the English thought better of it and sought to put their own man on the throne? That was madness, of course, a minor Lord of a mountain fastness no matter how well supplied with Enfields, could not be expected to force his wishes upon a kingdom, but still it argued that influence was being sought. It also meant that Otaro's position was very much more precarious than mine. By assaulting him, they had assaulted the authority of the Pope and by extension the Tycoon (or Shogun as Major Fitzpatrick referred to him), that coupled with his friends at court, meant that he was far too dangerous a man to have running about freely, if they let him live at all.

It did settle things on one score however. Lord Ide could not have had anything to do with Lord Hoji's murder. To do so would have attracted attention when he had a great deal to hide. It would have been the act of a madman or a fool. Cold comfort to us, but there was still the boy to think of. With Lord

Ide discounted as a captor, however, the chances of him being recovered alive seemed ever more remote.

I was taken from this maudlin reverie by the arrival of Major Fitzpatrick, who though a little red eyed did not seem overly inconvenienced by his overindulgence of the evening before. I stood with difficulty to receive him and he greeted me cordially, one might almost say slightly sheepishly as if he had realized that his conduct of the night before had been shameful and he was at pains to make good the fault.

"I was wondering, Captain, if you would do me the honour of joining me for breakfast?" And with those words, fine though Suki's broth was, I was ravenously hungry. He had also brought with him my kit, which had been patched and cleaned and no doubt gone through, but that was nothing for the moment. I excused myself, had Suki bring hot water, and felt the small joys of washing and shaving and having clean linen. I presented myself, feeling entirely civilized, some twenty minutes later.

Breakfast was an odd affair, eaten sitting in the courtyard, with its grim faced guards glowering at us over the toast, at a table covered with a white cloth and seated on chairs which like the table had been fashioned from Enfield crates. Major Fitzpatrick, his strange drawling accent now firmly back in place, guided me through the repast with evident pride. For a man alone in a strange land, he put out a magnificent spread. There were kippers and kedgeree, a sort of rice and fish collation which the Major assured me was as British as the Tower of London (not a simile I cared for much given the circumstances), followed by a sort of toast ("They're not bread eaters, Hood, it's not natural") with preserves and, joy of joys, real coffee produced with a flourish from a Fortnum and Mason's hamper. I have had more salubrious breakfasts, but few cups of coffee as dear to me as that one.

It was over breakfast that the Major began to make things clear. It was as if the events of the night before had never happened (or perhaps in his sodden state he'd forgotten them), he began by suggesting that Otaro was not who he claimed to be. "Now old boy, not wishing to cast aspersions on your judgement, but are you sure this Johnny of yours is really who he says he is? I mean how well do you really know him? You see, my chap Ide reckons that he's a charlatan, a con man of some stripe or other. Having talked to him, that is, he claims all sorts of things. I was wondering if you couldn't shed some light on it. You say Lord Hoji was killed and the heir kidnapped, which is what provoked the frightful attacks on Lord Ide's manor. Nasty business, but it's what your friend, your acquaintance rather, one can never really know one these chaps, not really, claims to be looking into, yes?"

I responded as heatedly as I dared that the murder of Lord Hoji was our only reason for being on Lord Ide's lands and that Otaro's bone fides were as solid as they could possibly be.

"I understand completely, Hood, what you quite honestly believe him to be, but one never really knows these people. I mean there were chaps during the Sepoy mutiny not two years ago, who swore blind that their boys were as God fearing and law abiding a regiment of soldiers of the Queen as you could ever come across, only to wake up the next morning to discover that every man jack of them had deserted to the mob in the night. You never can tell."

I didn't take kindly to this comparison between my comrade, who had never broken faith in his life to a mob of mutineers, but I let it pass, seeing an altogether more disturbing turn to the Major's conversation. I was about to rise to Otaro's defence when the Major continued "Of course you'll be able to plead his case in a moment, Lord Ide has asked to see you and I'm sure you'll be able to sort things out yourself. If you're sure that this Otaro chap is who he says he is of course...". He trailed off and the rest of the meal passed in small talk as I racked my brains to think of what evidence I could offer to establish Otaro's identity. I was still immersed in this when we were conveyed to the apartment of Lord Ide, during which I got some glimpse of his estate. The comparison with Lord Hoji's was not favourable, there was far too much gravel for my liking and far too few flowers and trees. While Lord Hoji's castle had had all the colour expected of the seat of an Oriental potentate, married to that simplicity that is uniquely Japanese, Lord Ide's manse was an altogether more grey affair. What was simple in Lord Hoji's castle was stark and spartan in Lord Ide's and the latter, lacked the former's warmth for all the sun it got. That Lord Hoji's had been a place of hospitality and the Lord Ide's a prison, no doubt coloured my perception, but still the difference was plain and I wondered, as I was guided through paper corridors without number, what such a difference might indicate about the respective characters of the men in question. And then almost without noticing it I was in the presence of the man himself.

The audience chamber was a large one, perhaps made of three or four rooms which had been opened out to create the larger space. The room was devoid of banners or any other sort of decoration that I had learned to associate with such chambers. Lord Ide was at one end, perched on a low stool on a raised dais, flanked by his chamberlain and retainers. A rank of samurai lined the walls on either side, each of whom was bearing one of Major Fitzpatrick's cherished Enfield muskets at port arms. I was quite startled by their appearance, which must have been given away by some movement of my face because Major Fitzpatrick gripped my wrist and whispered fiercely in my ear.

"Take no account of how it looks, man. Simply advance to the chap, stop three paces before him, bow and follow my lead. Do I make myself clear?"

I nodded and so we began to walk down the aisle, at a funereal step, the Major holding his sabre, I with my hands by my sides and my gaze fixed firmly to the front. It was well that it was so, for it took every ounce of my resolve to maintain a good front in spite of my injuries and to prevent myself from gaping at the extraordinary posse around me. Lord Ide himself was a man of middle years and almost hawklike spareness. His whiskers were sparse, but compensated by the extreme bushiness of his eyebrows and his hair was bound up in a topknot that shared the black - white, the "salt and pepper" appearance of the whole. His gaze was intense, his eyes slightly bulging and his thin mouth set. As he was seated it was difficult to guess his height, though I would reckon him at about the middle height, that is tall for a Japanese. His costume was as simple and spare as the man himself, of a faded, powder blue and he held himself in such stillness (a characteristic of the Japanese of rank) that I jumped when he suddenly barked a command and the ranks at either side of us sprang to attention, with a snap that would have done credit to the West Point drill team. While that did give me pause for a moment, the thing with which I had most difficulty I will explain in a moment.

While Lord Ide was every inch accoutered in the manner of a model samurai, his advisors were in no way as orthodox. The fellows at either side of him were dressed as samurai, but with the addition of black bowler hats, slightly shiny with wear, and while all wore the swords of their rank, one carried in his hands an umbrella of the Japanese sort but that had been painted black and had had to suffer the addition of a curved handle, so that it had the look of a London swell's umbrella. Several other members of the party affected bowlers, top hats and on two occasions shakos of a clearly British pattern. The Lord's command to attention had come as we had reached the halfway mark. It became clear that the guardsmen who were closer to him were of higher rank than those further away. They were fitted with outfits in the typical samurai cut, but topped with shakos except for those two nearest the Lord who were wearing the bearskins of grenadiers on their heads. These two men, titans by Japanese standards, maintained a most ferocious mien while straining the highly polished chinstraps of their immense hats by thrusting out their chins in a grotesque manner. Only later, did I realize that they were perhaps attempting to imitate the prodigious chin and matchless pugnacity of Major Fitzpatrick.

We stopped some three paces from the dais and bowed low, bending at the middle and I all the while keeping an eye on the Major, so as to follow his example. I paused, waiting to be addressed, when the Chamberlain (not, as it turned out, the fellow with the umbrella, but the other chap in the silk top hat), began a formal introduction which the Major translated to the best of his ability, (his Japanese was inferior to mine, but not by much) which made it clear that Lord Ide was a formidable man indeed and not to be trifled with. Then the Major introduced me, quoting particulars of my rank and background that could only have been gleaned from my journal, blast him. I noticed throughout the exchange, that as well as omitting the details that would have revealed his snooping in my journal the Major softened several of the Chamberlain's phrases. For all his evident respect for our skill at arms, Lord Ide still employed men who considered us barbarians.

There was some small talk, during which I complimented him on the turnout of his guard and thanked him for the kindness and medical attention that had been shown me.

"You see," said the Lord slowly, "you find yourself in a very unusual position, Captain. You are in my lands, in the company of a man who claims to be a high official of our government, a man who also attacked my men in the course of their duty. My lands are those of the interior of the country where foreigners are forbidden by writ of the Son of Heaven himself and who has written that those who breach this edict are to have their heads struck from their shoulders. Now if this fellow was the government official he claimed to be, he would have leave to grant you permission to travel with an escort. However, since he is obviously a charlatan, his permission is worthless and you find yourself unwittingly in breach of the law."

I protested at this as simply as I could, so as not to put more weight on the Major's limited store of Japanese than it would bear, asserting both my innocence and the genuineness of Otaro's rank, when the Lord cut me off.

"Though traditionally, Captain, ignorance of the law is no defence, I feel in your case it would be better to withhold judgement. The Major has vouched for your being a man of rank and good character and I will take his assurances on that regard. However, the severity of your companions crime is so great that it cannot go unpunished." I became heated at this point, arguing my case and Otaro's with every resource I had available to me. The Major softened some of my more ill-chosen words, even as he struggled to keep up.

"Haven't you found his seals of office or other marks of his ranks?" I asked.

"We have not", was the reply and the Lord countered with "also, Captain, though I can only conclude that you are ignorant of the ways of our country, but such a personage as this fellow claims to be would travel with an entourage and as many attendants as befits his station. It would be most inappropriate for him to travel on his own, without servants, even," he coughed, "even the company of such a man as yourself. You must admit that our conclusions are supported by the available evidence and that the contrary argument is supported only by his word and yours and sadly, Captain, it is clear that you are in no position to judge the right. However, so that mercy may temper justice, it has been decided that this miscreant is to be held, while you, spared as you were, by the quality of English powder", the major shot him an angry and incredulous look at this and did not translate the sentence in full, "shall be my guest until an escort can be arranged to convey you back to Yokohama. You are welcome to spend your recreation as you see fit, though due to the late unpleasantness I would ask that you refrain from venturing outside the castle without an escort. I could not possibly risk such a stain upon my hospitality as to allow harm to come to you while you are in my care. My chamberlain," "that's the bugger in the silk topper" interjected the still fuming Major, "or Major Fitzpatrick will see to your needs until then." And with that, we were dismissed.

13

*Late night roistering leads to a wretched discovery.
Major Fitzpatrick discourses on the affairs of nations.
I am condemned to death again.*

There followed a period of several days where I stayed in the confines of the castle closely watched by Suki who was at least a pleasant gaoler. She taught me to play a game not unlike checkers with small black and white pebbles. It was diverting, though she beat me soundly at every opportunity. The Major paid a call on me only once during those first few days, explaining that his duties called him away, but he kindly returned what remained of my kit and added something of his own small library. Of the three volumes, he pressed on me, the first two were turgid enough, but the last was a translation of the Three Musketeers by the Frenchman, Dumas, which was much better. I shall forever be in his debt for having introduced me to that author.

The days dragged and so I explored and sketched the castle as best I could, learning that I was in an outer part, surrounded by what would be called a curtain wall in a European castle. There was a central keep[27], was nothing more than a regular building heavily fortified and put up on a stone base surrounded by a

---
[27] Hood really mustn't have been paying attention in class at West Point, which specialized in military engineering, to use such an archaic term to describe a fortification.

wall, that I was barred from entering. My observations led me to a few conclusions; firstly that Otaro was probably being held within the confines of the inner wall and secondly, the black smudge that appeared on the horizon marked the death of another settlement to feed Lord Hoji's hatred which probably explained the Major's absence.

But, for the most part, I rested. It was clear that my fever had not truly left me, for I slept badly and woke often, my teeth chattering and my body bathed in a cold sweat. Strange dreams, the products of a brain addled by fever, came and went, though some of them remained clear in my memory, as few dreams ever had, before or since.

I dreamt oftentimes of my mother, which I suppose is understandable. She was a sign of happier times and of home. But I also had a curious dream that recurred several times. I would wake on my pallet, my eyes fixed on the ceiling. There was a wetness about my chest, so that I feared that I had been truly wounded. I would look down to survey the damage and see a vixen crouched by me. She was licking the bruises on my chest and when she felt my eyes on her, she would look at me. Her eyes were very dark and wet and as they met mine, I would feel drowsy. She would place her paw on the injured part, her claws pinching the skin and my eyes would shut, just for a moment.

I would wake again, not knowing that I was still dreaming, and she would be gone, but the bruises on my chest would have formed themselves in the imprint of a paw. That very same paw print that we had found on the ledge where Lord Hoji had met his death. I quite clearly remember examining the paw print on my chest, quite perplexed. I even examined my self in a mirror when I truly woke and thought myself half mad for doing so. Though perhaps, not as mad as I should have thought myself for feeling disappointed when, in the light of day, they were just plain old bruises.

It was very curious, but the rest did do me good and I healed fast.

The Major reappeared on the sixth day of my incarceration, looking drawn and pale, under his fiery red hair. He waved aside the thanks I offered for the books and sat down, calling for wine and generally cursing the Japanese as incompetents without peer. He made some rather choice comments about Lord Hoji and proceeded to massage his feet with evident satisfaction. I kept myself to small talk and waited for him to commit the first indiscreteion once liquor and loneliness had done their work. It wasn't long in coming.

I don't believe Major Fitzpatrick was a bad man, he was simply a soldier doing his duty. Though he never admitted much to me, he alluded to his being there in an official capacity several times. He was terribly lonely though and it was a weakness that I played on continually during the several weeks I spent in captivity. He was always caught between Scylla and Charybdis[28], his garrulous nature warring with his professional instinct to keep his mouth shut. In the end it was his vanity that was his undoing. Lord Ide's

---

28 Scylla and Charybdis in Greek mythology, two immortal and irresistible monsters who beset the narrow waters traversed by the hero Odysseus in his wanderings (later localized in the Strait of Messina). Encyclopedia Britannica, Standard Edition, 2005.

comment about the quality of English powder had infuriated him.

"The man's sharp enough, but not so much as to keep his own house in order, English powder my eye, he's running his own bloody powder mill outside the government monopoly and his own chaps were stealing from him and he's afraid that he'll be hounded by the Tycoon for breaking the monopoly, as if half the country wasn't doing it already."

I also learned that Lord Ide's retainers had been impressed by the coloured lithographs in the Major's manuals of arms and that was what had sparked the craze for European headgear. "So he comes to me and says he wants shakos, so a hat maker makes him a shako, but where the hell do you find a bearskin in bloody Japan? I ended up making a week long ride to buy them from a guinea bastard[29] in charge of a theatre company. I ask you."

We spent several nights together and I got more from him each time. Lord Hoji's men were tearing the countryside apart it seemed and with powder in short supply Lord Ide's men were having a hard time stopping them. So, the Major was reaping Ide's displeasure through no fault of his own. He was not a happy man.

During these interviews, as he became drunker I asked him for news of Otaro, only to be fobbed off with excuses about news from Yeddo. Only when the Major revealed on his fourth night in my company that he was going to be called away again, did

---

29 A pejorative term for an Italian, similar to eyetie or wop.

I become desperate enough to press him. He was a gregarious drunk, but prone to fits of ill temper.

"The poor bugger is fucked, Robert. Accept it and be thankful that your own bloody neck is safe, in no small part to my efforts thankyouverymuch. He had friends in Yeddo, that's true and he's very likely everything you say he is, but Lord Ide has friends in Yeddo too and they're probably of a very different stripe. Anyway, Lord Ide can't possibly own up to having horse whipped a naobab of the land, even if he was gadding about on his own in the middle of a small war. All this Tycoon business is so much stuff. They're worse than the bloody Commons at home. Ide's friends will give him the word about whether it's safe to top your friend and he'll be for the chop, sure as damn, and no-one will be any the wiser except you, who'll be chucked on the first boat out of Yokohama for straying about the place without a permit. And if you don't, old boy, well, that is another story." And he gave me a look that made it very clear what would happen if I didn't cooperate and allow my friend to be murdered.

"And that will be the end of Yankee impertinence", he laughed. "Well it will and don't come the high and mighty with me, fellow. You chaps were happy enough to take a slice of China when we cracked her open[30] and to look down your noses at us while you did it. If we didn't sell them the bloody opium some else would have. And you followed our example quick enough, drove a bloody great big steamship into the bay and it was c'mon Johnny

---

30 Major Fitzpatrick is referring the Opium War of 1840, where the British government invaded China after several British merchants were arrested when they refused to abide by the Chinese governments ban on opium importation. The invasion was deeply traumatic for the Chinese, who were soundly beaten and had to agree to a humiliating treaty that granted Britain extensive trading rights and the territory of Hong Kong.

Jap tradey tradey or chop chop, savy? You'll savy pretty quick my lad or I'll blow your bloody paper cities all to blazes."

I agreed that I wouldn't and he was absolutely correct, where upon he proclaimed me a capital fellow and began to sing "Rule Britannia" while lying on his back. Time was absolutely of the essence or all was lost, so for once I called Suki and motioned to her that the Major needed assistance. We carried him, still singing, to the keep, which was the very object. I must at all costs find Otaro, because if what the Major said was true then the return of a messenger from Yeddo was not deliverance but a death sentence. The major was growing maudlin as we carried him through the gate. Suki was stumbling under the weight, while I was treated to a condescending stare from the guard, one of Lord Ide's favourites, who seemed to convey in his gaze alone his disdain for me and all my race.

I was doing my best to ignore the Major, who was babbling about what a good sport I was, even as Suki was leading us in the direction of his quarters. I was casting about for some clue as to the place of Otaro's captivity. "Poor bugger," mumbled the Major, "doesn't seem right, jus' killin' him would be cleaner. Your little yellow friend, Hood." I laid him against a pillar, for we were still outside and repeated his word, "Yes poor fellow indeed, my little yellow friend Major, where is he, may I see him?" I had to repeat myself several times to be understood and ignore Suki's protestations which were becoming quite animated until the Major snapped at her in Japanese and she suddenly became quiet. " Poor bugger, well you may as well look at him, but you won't like it." And with a sudden lurch, he shambled away under his own power, Suki following behind, hopping from foot to foot in her nervous anxiety and turning to me with looks that were beseeching and accusatory by turns. The major stumbled and staggered through the darkness and how we didn't raise the whole estate I wonder to this day. I suppose that they were used to the Major drunkenly crashing about and simply tolerated him as he was the source of all things Enfield and concerning the percussion cap. We passed several other guards, who with their swords and guns and ridiculous hats, looked like banditti from a comic opera. The incongruity of it would have made me laugh out loud, if the Major hadn't led us past the stables and towards a sight that banished all levity from my mind.

I had taken a paper lantern from the stables as we passed it and felt in my pockets for matches as soon the horrible stench assailed us. The smell was beyond endurance. It wasn't simply the homely smells of the stable, but the acrid biting scent of exposed human filth and sweat. The major had fallen to his knees at this point, still clutching his sake bottle and was crawling forward in the dim light, muttering to me. "Careful, Robin or ye'll fall in, strike a light there man, strike a light." Suki had backed away her hand across her mouth in horror as soon as she had caught wind of it and now stood, wringing her hands with worry by the stable door. I cursed and struggled with the lamp and I had almost succeeded in lighting it when I nearly dropped it in astonishment.

"Captain Robert, is that you?" came a low urgent whisper. "Otaro?" I called back, then caught myself and brought my voice down low. "Where are you, man?" "He's in the bloody hole, are you blind?" retorted the major and rolled over on his back to remonstrate with me. The sudden movement convinced him of the need of a restorative swig from his bottle, by which time I had fallen to my knees and was crawling towards him. "Captain, no light, if you please, it would only attract attention. Mr. Fitzpatrick visits me on occasion, but he is rarely in a position to make a light". As I reached the major all became clear, he was lying at the edge of a pit. It was round and some four feet in diameter and from it emanated, as I have said before, the very worst of smells. I peered over the edge and saw nothing but darkness, so deep was the pit and though I thought I saw movement, Otaro's position was still obscure to me.

"Otaro, how deep is the pit? Can you climb out?

"Not at present Captain Robert", he rejoined somewhat testily, "but listen. You must escape from this place. Lord Ide's care makes it clear that we are without hope if we remain here. He has powerful friends who are against the Shogun and sees me as a threat. I am lost, Captain, but if you stay here you are lost too. These are desperate men."

I grew a little impatient at this and snapped back that we would be leaving together, but if I could beg his damned pardon, how deep was the hole? There followed a silence and then a simple response, "impossibly, but since you ask it is thirty feet deep and shaped liked a...," he hesitated and said a Japanese word that I did not know.

"Shaped like a what?" I said, growing fiercer.

"A...a....a.." he stammered "...like a medicine bottle, your green one."

I thought quickly and called it to mind, "a shape with three sides? But a circle?"

"Yes", he responded, "one of those", "a cone". "Oh" he said and was then silent, until he piped up again, "also please understand Captain that I am shackled".

"On the hands or on the feet?"

"The hands".

"Well, there's nothing to be done right now, but hold fast, help is on the way."

"If you say so Captain Robert" he answered in a voice so unlike that of my friend that despair stabbed at my heart. There and then, but for the sodden stirring of the major, I would have given way to my fears. I lifted him and carried him to Suki who was still watching white faced from the stable corner. The major's apartment was a little distance away. It was a small room with a sleeping mat, a few books, mostly drill manuals and a bible, a miniature in the old style since made extinct by the daguerreotype[31] showing a stern woman of middle years, lay

---

31 An early form of photography. Quite expensive at the time.

by his bedside. By the chin I can only assume she was some relation, probably his mother.

Suki laid him on the mat and began to remove his boots, which had tracked mud across the floor and he started again and murmured. "Terrible thing, old boy, putting him in a hole like that. Worse than you chaps with a nigger, leaving him there with shit all over him. Wouldn't, couldn't do it to a nigger." He rolled over, patted Suki on the behind with a sort of beatific smile on his face, told her she was a good girl and fell asleep. For my part, I looked around to see if there was anything worth stealing that would aid us in our escape. Shameful I know, but there was nothing there that would not have brought with it immediate discovery. I returned to my quarters down at heart, but convinced that escape was now an absolute necessity and that my friend, however much he seemed beaten in spirit, could and would be rescued.

14

More roistering.
A most unusual ally.
The recovery of honour or at least steel.
A nocturnal excursion with a most unlooked-for end.

And so it fell to me, over the next few days, to see what could be done. It had an electric effect on me and stirred me from the lethargy that imprisonment had begun to bring on. I walked about a great deal, studying the castle as I had before, but now with a purpose and that made all the difference. I watched the guards at their work and they weren't up to much. I played the pebble game with Suki, still improving not a jot and prevailed upon her to feed me more heartily than she had before. I ate heavily, fattening myself for the privations that I knew were to come and made a hole in the floor of the sliding closet in my room and there stored what rice and fish I could, wrapped in pages torn from my journal. The days passed and the essential problems of our captivity became clear to me.

Firstly, there was the matter of the castle itself, which was divided into an inner and outer part, lying on a spit of rock that was thrust out from the mountain like a promontory into the sea. So, it was surrounded on three sides by a sheer drop and on the fourth by a high wall, which was patrolled. The second matter was that of Otaro's prison. A rope was the only thing for it, as he could not possibly climb out due to its shape. Its proximity to the stables was an advantage though, as there rope could certainly be found and perhaps tools with which to strike his bonds and defend ourselves. The trick of course, once Otaro was free and out of the hole, would be in escaping the castle. My appearance and his unique odour would prevent any attempt at bluffing our way out of the outer or inner gates. We must scale the wall and make our way on the narrow ledge that ran along the outside of the wall until we reached the broader space that led to the main gates.

These were days of anxious expectation and subterfuge. I was not summoned to speak with Lord Ide further though the major had asked me before he left to write analysis of Lord Hoji's force, more to keep me occupied than for any other reason. He felt responsible for me, even though I had complicated his mission, as I was helpless and of his own people. I grew to pity rather than scorn his recourse to drink. In return for the few small kindnesses he could pay me, I made it my business to be good company. On the third day of his second absence, I heard the crash of a volley, a valley or so distant and again there was a smoky smudge in the sky. I prayed for his safe return, not least because he was the only avenue of escape for either myself or Otaro.

And Providence delivered him to us. Two days later, at the head of a company of Lord Ide's men ostensibly under the command of one of the bearskinned buffoons, he was galvanised by victory and his face was as flushed as his coat. His humour was so good and his excitement so great, that it was the only time I heard him speak in his own accent while sober.

"We thrashed them Robert, thrashed them fairly lively, the lads were grand and stood their ground and loaded and fired like guardsmen. Oh mercy! Would that you had seen it? It was a bad day for the cavalry and no mistake."

"Prisoners?" I asked, eager for news of what might have happened in Lord Hoji's lands in our absence, but I was disappointed.

"Not a sausage, old boy. Most of them got away, worse luck, but twenty dead and one fellow so badly shot through the vitals that he was given leave to cut his own stomach open before they chopped his bloody head off. We took some good horses. Have a look for yourself."

I busied myself for the rest of the day seeing to the horses that the Major had taken. All were in a state of neglect and several had wounds, which were seen to. Unfortunately, I could see no way of stealing a pair (I cursed the loss of my dear Rocinante now!) to aid in our escape. I was summoned from the stables by Suki as the day was drawing in. She had prepared a meal for Edward and I in my quarters and would I please come?

Major Fitzpatrick was as expansive in triumph as he was in wine and as the meal wore on I began to worry that this would be one of the rare nights he would not overindulge. But as I pressed him for details and refilled his glass, both tale and wine flowed.

Lord Hoji's men had been raiding Lord Ide's land without pause since the first attack that had cost poor Jingen so dear. Ide had lost few men, only those samurai who were in the villages at the time. They were most often cut down in the initial rush, whereupon Lord Hoji would burn the village and move on. Three of Lord Ide's villages had been razed in such a manner and the peasantry were panicking.

"That's what really put the wind up him, dear boy, the samurai aren't bloody likely to take in the harvest themselves are they? Once Ide realized what Hoji's game was, he got very lively indeed and start demanding things right and left. It all must be stopped by a useless shower of samurai, a cast off like meself and two hundred lads with that many cartridges to rub between them. Something must be done old boy, something must be done. I left the gallant hatters to do as they wished as they won't take orders from me for they're insolent bastards. I took out a platoon to go hunting myself. Kaito who you saw leading the lads in, proud as a rooster, went with me. He's not a bad lad and knows to do what he's told."

I complimented him on the address of his troops, but he just smiled and carried on.

"You must call me Edward and anyway, they were first rate. Of course, Hoji had gotten all cosy murdering villagers and stuck to the same damn plan. Everything time he'd have a quick spy to check that the coast is clear and then charge in. Of course, by the time he got to my village, he'd so much brass that he didn't even stop to have a look and just charged straight in. The man's a plunger[32] and worse than our lot in Russia. Of course we were waiting for him. We let him hit the village, there was no harm in it. All the locals had cleared off. So we let him blow his horses, popped out and nabbed him against the river. The silly bugger tried to charge straight back through, but my boys were having none of it. They stood firm, gave him two volleys and then the bayonet. If they hadn't found the ford, we'd have bagged the lot."

And such it seemed was the day for the cavalry. At this point in the proceedings, Edward grew really quite exuberant and began to list the many sterling fighting qualities of his boys. I bore the lot patiently, waiting for my chance.

When finally, though it felt like an age, Edward's eyes began to drop and he began to mumble through his whiskers. I secured my secret store of rice and stowed my necessities that I could about my person, before summoning Suki. We bore the sleeping man through the gates, which were unusually lightly manned, perhaps I hoped because the gallant hat society were drowning their sorrows at having failed where Edward had succeeded. Or perhaps they were simply sheltering from the spattering rain that had begun to fall an hour before, I never learned why, but I was profoundly thankful for it. We conveyed Edward to his quarters when a terrible temptation was put before me. As I laid him down on the mat and Suki removed his boots, I saw that, in

---
32 British army slang for an overconfident cavalry officer.

breach of custom, his sword had not been stowed at the audience chamber, but was lying by his few personal effects.

I was unlikely to have another chance to get a weapon. I knelt there over the sleeping man, regarding the sword and wrestling with my conscience. It might be the difference between life and death for Otaro and I, but could I dishonour a man who had, as much as his duty allowed, been a friend to me. On one side life, and on the other, honour and friendship. But the choice was taken from my hands in a most curious manner. I tore my eyes from the sword for a moment, only to realize that Suki had fled the room, in which moment a sweat broke out on my brow. She knew all, she had divined all and was now at this very moment summoning the gallant hats, comical though they were, who would kill me easily. I was frozen with fear and unable to decide to do when Suki returned alone bearing a green bundle. She knelt by Edward's bed and looking at me openly, lifted his sword with difficulty and moved it to his right side, whereupon she shook her head so emphatically that I believe I copied her without thinking. She pressed the bundle into my hands and I drew it open, suppressing a cry of astonishment when I found it held two swords. One was Otaro's and the other had been the gift of old Hisamatsu. I gazed at her in wonderment and thanked her, when she spoke, in Japanese.

"Thank you, but, why?"

"They are yours. Go now, there is little time."

"But will you not be punished?"

"Perhaps, but he is my man and I am his and tonight my Lord will not punish him or me."

I was about to argue, when she shook her head again and turning from me as if I had left already, lay down beside Edward. There was nothing for it but to take her bounty and run. I found tools and rope in the stables and was in a matter of moments peering over the edge of Otaro's stinking prison. I could hear his sleeping sighs in the dark, and couldn't wake him with words. I was fit to tear my hair out, when I had an idea and tied a horseshoe to the rope and lowered it into the hole. I then swung it wildly about in the hope of striking him.

He woke with a sudden grunt of pain. "Otaro," I whispered, "grab the rope".

"What rope? Captain Robert, is that you? Who struck me?"

"I did, the rope is in the hole, now grab the rope and let's get out of here."

"Could you not simply have called out?"

"I did, now take the rope and be thankful for small mercies."

And it was in that spirit, blinking and reeking that Otaro emerged from the hole, his round familiar face now gaunt with hunger, his body weak and his skin pale. I was glad to see him, though it pained me to see him so obviously low in spirit. I had expected the prospect of escape to animate him, but he merely looked at me, shivering in the rain and the cold air of night. I thought for the first time that perhaps our escape was not so easy as first I thought.

"Come man, hurry or we are lost," and I dragged him after me by the sleeve. We retreated into the shadows by the stable and I knelt down, coiling the rope around my fore arm as I did so.

"Are you injured" I asked, looking about us.

"No" he shook his head slowly, his daze lifting, but being replaced by fearful glances that did little to reassure me.

I finished my business with the rope, tying it into a lariat ready to throw over the wall, while the poor fellow fretted with his hands and began to shift himself anxiously. I could not think what to do and all relied on me now. Swift action was vital or we would be taken.

"Otaro," I said "we are going to have to go over the wall. The way through the gates is heavily patrolled, but if we get over the wall, we can work our way along the ledge at its bottom and then gain the path to the road. Do you understand? It will be hard, but we can do it."

He nodded dumbly again and I despaired.

"I will help you, are you strong enough?"

I gave him one of my rice cakes and he ate almost without removing the paper. I cursed myself for not having foreseen this possibility. What else could be expected of this man, the proud, noble companion of mine, who had been starved, beaten, utterly humiliated, robbed of all the accustomed dignity of his class and more than that, the dignity of a man. I wished that I had brandy or had taken some of Edward's sake to revive his spirits and put fire in him. I thought of returning to Edward's quarters to get some but that would have been madness.

The difficulties that still faced us were daunting. The castle, though it was more of a walled estate house compared to the castle of Lord Hoji which had been built in the old warring days, was surrounded on three sides by a precipice. The cliff face dropped down some twenty rods[33] into the river below. Thus, there was only one means of getting to safety, the trail leading to the castle gate. Only the walls of the outer keep were wide enough to bear a parapet, the masons trusting to the great drop and the difficulty of getting past the outer keep for their security. The walls of the inner keep were neither particularly high, - about fifteen feet, nor were they particularly thick, only eighteen inches. These outer walls were not flush with the edge of the precipice. The builders who obviously didn't want to risk losing the entire wall to a few inches subsidence, had left a ledge of three feet at the foot of the wall. It wasn't enough for an attacker, but certainly enough for two fugitives who needed to bypass all the gates and guards and get to the causeway undetected. We might, of course, be spotted by the guards there, but that was a risk that we were going to have to run. All this I explained to Otaro, who was completely ignorant of the layout of the castle, but nodded again slowly.

It was maddening to see him thus and I felt the same sick feeling I had felt leading my first charge in Mexico, completely

[33] A rod is 16.5 feet, so approximately three hundred and thirty feet.

unsure of how my boys would hold up. I had to do something, anything to put heart in the man because he was utterly at sea. I grasped him by the shoulder and he looked at me suddenly.

"Otaro, it's this or death, understood? We both must prevail or perish. Are you with me?"

It was poor melodramatic stuff and I felt a little foolish after I'd said it, but he held himself a little straighter and I saw the ghost of a smile, the faintest shadow of the old boy, and I smiled myself, despite our circumstances. "Until death then, Captain Robert," he replied and everything was possible again. I passed him the bundle and showed him the spot where we would cross over the wall. It was three quarters along the wall of inner keep, where the mass of the main building would screen us from the tower marking the junction of the inner and outer walls. Getting there would take care, but going any closer or further would have brought even greater hazard.

The central work, Lord Ide's house, was an extraordinary structure, a towering pagoda of six storeys, set on a stone base that would have given even modern guns a run for their money. It was possible to see the top storey, a small look out tower, silhouetted in the dim light of the moon, but impossible to tell if it was manned. The roofs were not covered in the usual clay tiles, but in wooden ones covered with a sort of black lacquer that glistened in the rain and moonlight like the scales of a serpent.

There were still some wandering about on their Lord's business or private errands, but all that could be done was to trust to our luck. Our route was in shadow, most, but not all of the way and we would need to be swift. I explained as much to Otaro and we began our approach slithering on our bellies like redskins through the bushes and collections of stone that furnished Lord Ide's poor gardens. As we neared the wall, I realized that I had forgotten something. The part of the wall I had chosen for us to cross had nothing on it that I could lasso. Otaro seemed confused at this and told me that we would climb. "But I am no climber" said I. "Then I shall climb and bring the rope and you can climb that" he responded, more his old commanding self. I could not but agree.

Otaro took the rope from me and we crept forward with only the shadow and the rain to screen us. Otaro paused for a moment and at the base of the wall, took a breath and scaled it so quickly that I couldn't believe my eyes. He lay across the top of the wall and then dropping suddenly over the edge, which made me start and gave me an unpleasant presentiment of what lay over the wall. I lay there counting the seconds and adjusting Suki's bundle on my back, knowing that, quiet as we were, a sentry had but to turn his head look for a moment in an unaccustomed quarter and we were done. The rope flew over and its gentle slap on the stone work sounded like a whip crack to my straining ears. I crawled forward and taking a firm grip I scurried up the rope. I was only a few feet from the ground when I felt the rope give a little under my weight and scrambled up the rest with the speed of a gymnast.

It was there that our luck ran out. The first shot roared in the night above the rain and cracked against the wall by my side, another rang out and I tumbled over the wall. I have faced bayonets and bullets, charged only to see guns unmasked before me and faced death from enemies, starvation, thirst and disease, but the yawning chasm that opened up before my eyes as I fell over that wall lives forever in my nightmares.

I fell, hands out, the cliff stretched out beneath me, the river shining slick in the moonlight, down, down, down below. I screamed, utterly unmanned as if for an age, all fear of the bullets gone, as I fell headlong into the endless drop.

I came against the cliff side with a jerk that knocked all the wind out of me as Otaro reached out and grabbed the bundle at my back and lying flat on his back, held me there at the ledge, suspended. I looked down as I dangled over the precipice and lost all articulacy, as Otaro strained under my weight. With strength surprising in such a small man, even more so after his ordeal, he dragged me over the edge until I lay at the base of the wall, stretched out and shaking with fright. I fought to compose myself and did so sufficiently to realize that Otaro was talking to me in a low voice and that people were shooting at us.

I stood unsteadily on the ledge, facing the wall because to do otherwise would be to invite paralysis. We began to step sideways along the ledge as quickly as we dared, Otaro encouraging me all the way. There were shouts and a cacophony of ringing bells inside the walls and we quickened our pace. The wall hove in near the gate, widening the ledge to comparatively roomy three or four yards and I made for that. As we moved more swiftly there were slips and stomach wrenching jerks as I nearly slipped in the wet grass of the ledge several times. We were some forty yards from our point when the first guard appeared and lowered his rifle. There was a bang and a cloud of smoke. Though the bullet went wide, I did not hear it. We lay down on the ledge as more guards appeared and began to form a line, banging away at us like boys at a fair.

"Captain Robert, they are not very good shots. We will be here all night."

They were high, common enough in inexperienced marksmen, but they'd soon rouse the Major and we'd be shot like partridge. "It is a pity we cannot rush them, Captain Robert. I would have liked to have died with my father's sword in my hand".

"There Sir, I can oblige you" said I as another shot smashed the stonework above us. I rolled over onto my back and undid the bundle, drawing out the two swords. Otaro actually laughed with pleasure and so did I, to hear that sound again, even at that time, even in that place.

"Thank you Captain Robert, thank you very much, you are a swell fellow", he said as he hefted the blade. I took my own and held it in front of me. It was far lighter than my sabre and it felt almost ghostlike in my hand. I looked at the line, who were now firing volleys, poor ones at that, but more dangerous that random shots. The crew that fired at us were members of the gallant hat brigade. The common troops, drilled by Major Fitzpatrick, would have riddled us in moments.

"Let us rush them then, Captain Robert" said Otaro and I agreed. We crept forward, swords drawn, Otaro pausing only to retie the bundle on my back. The rain was slackening now and the gallant hats who had been lost in a pall of their own making were revealed by a gust of wind. Otaro was close at my heels when I realized that one of the swine, who was presuming to give orders to the others, was waving my sabre about and had my pistol tucked into his girdle, bold as you please. We crawled on covered by the smoke, volleys crashing over our heads. It was hopeless of course, even if we felled a few of the gallant hats, there were more competent troops forming behind them. But at least it was better than disgrace or captivity. The precipice to my left no longer concerned me, fear was past. We were fighting only for honour now. I wondered fleetingly about my mother and what news might reach her, if any, of my end. I commended my soul to the Lord and when Otaro gave the word, we rose and charged. I made for where the fellow who had thieved my sabre, knowing that I would receive a bullet in the breast before I reached him, but wanting something to aim for. The wall grated against my shoulder and behind me, Otaro uttered a piercing shriek, a sort of shrill keening, when the smoke parted I saw the party not twenty feet from us, dumbstruck. Some turned to run, others struggled to reload, the swine fumbled with my pistol and I felt a grim pagan joy rise in me as I screamed a battle cry. You fellow, I will die here, but I will end you too so help me God.

And that's what I was shouting when Otaro pushed me off the ledge.

15

We survive, we regroup, we set out again.

He informed me afterwards that he had not told me of his plan because, as he understood it, I was a Christian and therefore forbidden to commit even an entirely honourable suicide. He had thought the chance so slim that it was tantamount to death and he did not want to present me with a choice that might give me religious qualms, but rather took the thing upon himself. As he said later, "I could always take comfort in the thought, Captain Robert, though in truth the time for contemplation would have been short, that I had at least tried to save you and in doing so, I had not taxed your conscience, having taken the trouble to kill you myself." It was a thought that gave him immense satisfaction he said, to be able to repay the many kindnesses I had done him.

I shall pass over my response here. Suffice to say that his reasoning did not comfort me, when I was pulled, shivering and blank eyed with terror, from the water. I believe that I fainted. I have never been able to recall the details of the fall, my first coherent memory being lying at the waters edge panting furiously and attempting to lever myself up with my sword, which I held clasped in a death grip. Otaro lay beside me similarly winded.

It was only after several minutes that we could recoup enough to look around. The rain was hard, biting through our thin clothes and I could not stop my teeth chattering, but I did look around enough to realize that we were some way, down-stream from the castle. I would have lost it all there, slept where I lay, so overcome was I with nervous shock, had not Otaro roused me and through a series of patient orders got us both moving further from the castle. We marched on for an interminable time. I thought of nothing. Keeping hold of my bundle and my sword were my sole responsibilities and I fixed on those ideas to the exclusion of all else. When we finally fell down, we were deep in the forest and so utterly spent that we would have been incapable of resisting a pursuer anyway.

I awoke the next morning to find my entire body a mass of bruised flesh and aching bone. I had sustained a fearful battering in the river and my welts and scrapes were legion. The ground was still glistening wet from the rain of the night before, but the sun at least was high in the sky and beating down with a warmth that brought some life back to our bodies. It was against all the odds, but we were alive, the knowledge of it stunned me. I had not realized how resigned I had become to my death. I lay there listening to the myriad sounds of the forest, thanking God for our deliverance and the absence of pursuit.

Otoaro was stretched insensible under the same tree I had been under and I thought it best not to wake him yet, but instead sorted through the bundle Suki had given me, which proved my anchor the night before. There were scabbards for our swords.

My poor cakes of rice, were now sodden, but were still wrapped in their cartridge paper. There was some pickled fish and some shards of pottery which I guessed had been an earthenware container broken in the fall. Eventually I woke Otaro, who had also been beaten raw by the night's adventures and we devoured a breakfast of rice and fish. Only after that did I question him as to our location.

"We are to the north of Lord Ide's castle. I thought it the least likely direction of pursuit as any party sent after us will assume that we would head straight for Lord Hoji's lands. Though there may not be any pursuit at all. Any reasonable man will assume that we were been killed by the fall." I nodded, suppressing the disquiet thoughts of the night that before brought to my stomach.

"So what is the plan then?" I asked. "We are no closer to accomplishing our mission than we were four weeks ago". Otaro nodded and fell to thinking about it, while I gathered our few supplies together and we talked it over in the warmth of the sun. It was clear that whatever his other faults Lord Ide was not responsible for Lord Hoji's death. The new Lord's onslaught had taken him by surprise and anyway, there was no chance of the gallant hats ambushing the procession with swords or bringing only a dozen men. Otaro confirmed it. He had been questioned at length as to what caused the sudden belligerency of Lord Hoji and had answered truthfully in the hope of proving his innocence. I had talked the matter over with Edward who had been equally ignorant of Lord Hoji's demise until I had enlightened him. They were in the clear.

There was also the added complication of Major Fitzpatrick's presence as well as the Enfield rifles, both of which seemed to point to either an official British interest in the region, whether mercantile or military. In any case the latter is so often a cover for the former that they can generally be considered the same. Otaro was greatly exercised that a private person, even one so elevated as Lord Ide, would take it upon himself to have secret dealings with a foreign power. His anger was only further stoked when I told him about the Major's indiscreet comments to me about the prospective reshuffle.

So our duty was clear and we arrived at a plan. We must first return to Lord Hoji's castle as he was the closest thing we had to an ally in these parts. From there Otaro would dispatch a message to Yeddo detailing Lord Ide's perfidy and urging vigorous action on the part of the government. He said that he might gain Lord Hoji's support in this as the bellicose nobleman would most certainly be eager to back any course of action that might justify his actions after the fact.

"So in aiding you, he clears himself into the bargain."

"True, and gains merit by being seen to have acted as soon as it came to his attention. He is a mad dog, Captain. He would not have started an unsanctioned war with Lord Ide on the flimsiest of evidence, if he was not a mad dog. But he is not a fool. I will convince him that it will be to his advantage."

"And as to our other mission?" I suppose I should have been more concerned about the fate of nations, but I have always been sentimental.

"It remains undone and my promise to Lady Hoji remains unfulfilled. But we do no good here without provisions or succour and we will have to re-equip ourselves before deciding what course of action to take. We do little good to Lady Hoji while we are starving and there may have been developments in our absence. Perhaps the child has been found or returned."

"Perhaps," I said, though I thought it unlikely. I was glad that neither his ordeal, nor the treachery of Lord Ide had driven our mission from his head. With that settled, we rose to go and I watched Otaro carefully. Despite his sangfroid, he was still weak and Ide's prison had left its mark upon him. I carried what supplies we had and we were about to head off when an idea struck me.

"Otaro, the route we took last night, was uphill was it not?' Parallel to Lord Hoji's castle and to the north of Lord Ide's?"

He agreed that is was, but seemed puzzled since we had discussed the matter after breakfast. "Might it be better not to take the direct route, but to make for Master Sum's home, which is closer. He may have horses and he will certainly have food. We will be able to get to the castle faster with full bellies.

Otaro agreed that is was a better idea than a straight run for the castle and I felt glad that I had paid close attention to the country on the trip out. I knew the general area and Master Sum had given Otaro definite instructions during their last interview. Between us we would work it out.

It was a slow day, with frequent stops, mainly to save Otaro's limited strength and to refresh ourselves wherever we found water. As we had no means of carrying it we had to take as we found it. We had travelled eight miles by my estimation, when the heavens dumped rain on us in prodigious quantities. Mindful of Otaro's health (and my own) I decided on a break for lunch and we sat beneath a huge beach tree eating our cold rice and the few remaining scraps of fish. If I was right, if we made another five miles, we might, barring accidents, make Master Sum's home by noon of the following day. As the rain continued and we sat staring at the greyness of it, Otaro spoke.

"Thank you, Captain Robert."

"You're welcome, though it's poor fare. Master Sum will lay a much better table, I'll warrant."

He paused for a moment and displaying that reticence that is as natural to the oriental as breathing, he sighed.

"I mean to thank you for coming back for me at the waterfall and in the castle."

I flushed a bit at this, embarrassed.

"Think nothing of it. What I did was for your friendship and my honour. I could not have left you even if I wanted to. Anyway I have you to thank for my standing here today. If you hadn't pushed me from that cliff edge (oh Lord, that thought again) I would not be here, would I?"

"But you did not shrink from it, Captain Robert. I salute you. It was good to be by your side."

I stammered at this, not sure what to say, but he went on. "Unlike you Captain, I have never been in a battle before, though I think now I have some idea of what it might be like. And."

"And you did very well", I said cutting in. This was all too intimate and self congratulatory for me. Otaro was a fine fellow and had done well, but was obviously labouring under some mental burden that he lacked the language to express. It was for the best as no good ever comes of talking about such things. I rose and walked about a bit, studying the rain while my companion fell silent. I fidgeted, which spoiled my good humour and I was trying to hold myself erect and still, when Otaro spoke again.

"You will not find it as uncomfortable if you wear it in the belt rather than stowed in the bundle, Captain Robert." He said.

"Allow me," and he took my sword, old Hiramatsu's gift from the bundle and cut some rope from the binding so that he had enough to form a belt around my waist. I did not speak, as I was a little shocked, having remembered Otaro's previous prohibition. He slid the blade into the belt and set it so I could rest my hand on it.

"Remember," he said, "blade up, not quite what you are used to, though the draw should be the same across the body, like so."

He demonstrated by drawing his own sword and returning it to the scabbard with a lightning swiftness that belied my estimation of his health. He nodded, "Now you."

We spent some little time beneath the dripping evergreen as Otaro observed my stance and draw. It was strange, that class beneath the wide canopy as the rain spattered around us. I found the two handed grip very queer. The sword was too light for it, completely unlike my lost sabre. Otaro handed me his and though the two swords seemed almost identical to my eyes, the weights and balance were very different, amazing since they were so alike in every other respect. Otaro bound up his sleeves with the cord from his sash and showed me the proper two handed grip and had me copy him. I never mastered it and I maintain that while a western swordsman will perhaps need three or four blows to down his man (unless he's on horseback in which case it's a case of giving him the point and pressing on, rather than staying and fencing like a fool), he may get the opportunity to do so before the Japanese has made the one perfect strike that he needs, but only if he is lucky. After an hour, the rain softened and went and we moved on, Otaro smiling at me as he let down his sleeves.

"I will never make a good student, shall I? Mr. Fencing Master?"

"No, you are far, far too old", he said with a laugh, "though your American tricks would probably confuse a proper swordsman long enough for me to rescue you."

And we laughed at this a great deal.

16

***A fight. A reunion.
Our first real clue.***

Between the two of us, we had worked out that Master Sum's home was one day's march from where we were and once we had an object we set to it with a will. It was hard going, pushing up the mountain towards the lake of which he had told me. One advantage was that most of the peasants lived in the valleys and we were untroubled by observers. We did come across one village whose inhabitants had obviously fled the raiding forces of Lord Hoji. We saw their tracks on the trails, the bare footprints of men and women, children and handcarts. There were signs here and there, broken crockery or a scrap of fabric, which told us of their piteous flight. The shattered remnants of a poor but happy domesticity touched even my hardened heart and I felt my hatred for Lord Hoji grow all the more. That Lord Ide was a cruel man, made him no better in my eyes, since Lord Hoji inflicted this severity out of pique and desire for revenge rather than from any necessity. I am not so naïve as to think that war cannot be anything but cruel. I have been in its agent and sometimes its victim, but that it should happen without just cause is abominable.

We reached the deserted village late in the day and thought it best to stay the night there, as we would be crossing the border between the domains soon and it would be best to make that journey just before sun up. We rested the night in a small house that was poor but clean, a characteristic that immediately distinguishes the Japanese peasant from the Mexican peon, whose quarters are always indescribably filthy. We had the frugal fruits of a kitchen garden to enjoy and a roof over our heads and thought ourselves lucky men. I gave thanks to the Lord for his many blessings and we slept, with Otaro taking first watch.

Sadly, the privations of the previous days had taken their toll on me. I offer this as no excuse, but rather as an honest explanation for my conduct, which was inexcusable. During the middle watch, I fell asleep at my post on the porch of the small house with Otaro snoring inside wrapped in two mats. I remember that the weariness of the road had been lying very heavily on me, so I shook myself and rose and walked a beat so as to stay awake, only sitting down when my tiredness became intolerable. In an effort to stave off my exhaustion I drew out my journal, which, though wet, was still serviceable and set myself the work of recording what had happened in the last few days.

I was sitting there, with my journal on my knees when I slipped suddenly into a dream. I did not know it immediately, but soon my head drooped and I lifted it to see a fox standing in the centre of the kitchen garden. Though I am a city boy I knew she was a vixen, such is the logic of dreams. She gazed at me intently, her head poking out from amid the cabbages, her strange dark eyes shining. Stepping daintily between the plants she padded over to me, stopping only inches away. I felt the whisper of her breath against my skin and put my journal to one side and smiled when she placed a paw, with the elegant condescension of a lady of quality, in my hand. It was small and very warm, the pads rough against my palm. She sniffed me in an engaging sort of way and seemed to be waiting for something, when she started and suddenly bit my hand.

I woke with a jolt and heard a yell through the trees. My hand leapt to my sabre, I mean my sword. My journal had fallen from my lap and I caught it up and thrust it into my shirt. I was near panic, how long had I been asleep? Were we discovered? I dashed into the house and shook Otaro awake. He awoke slowly, so worn down was he by our escape, but he leapt up when the second yell came. We moved fast, Otaro grabbing our bundle while I watched the road and then we both made for the trees. We ran for nearly a minute then dropped panting in the shadow of a fir. We waited, willing our hearts to be still, when we heard men passing through the trees.

The men ahead of us were nervous at least, for I heard shouting and the crashing of branches in the dark. It was not the earnest manly yell of the hunter, but the concerned and beseeching cry of one who finds himself alone in the dark, abandoned by his comrades and who wishes very much that he could rejoin them.

Otaro and I lay in cover a little distance from the houses. We waited and, sure enough, we heard a panicked scrabbling on the other side of a nearby copse of trees. We drew our swords and braced ourselves for the coming battle, when much to our surprise we heard a crash, a frightened whinny and then an immense snapping and smashing of boughs as Jingen bestride my Rocinante exploded from the undergrowth hotly pursued by a horseman whose livery, even in the dim light, we could identify as Lord Ide's. We sprang from our cover, anxious to help our friend, and ran along the path at full tilt only to see them disappear around a bend in the road. We ran on, Otaro falling behind as his weakened constitution told, but I pushed on eager to find Jingen and regain my horse. Suddenly Rocinante, her eyes wide and her lips and flanks flecked with foam, hammered past us, throwing me off my feet and knocking the wind from me. As I regained my footing I yelled for Otaro to stick with Jingen, that I would deal with Lord Ide's man. Plucking up my sword from where it had fallen, I moved into the trees, hoping to take the man by surprise.

   I need not have bothered, for as I slowed, I could hear the man swearing and his horse whinnying in some obvious discomfort. I reached the point where the forest broke, only to see that the trail had been blocked by an abandoned tumbril[34], about which were scattered the relics of a fleeing populace, blankets, baskets and all the rest. But the strangest sight was that of Lord Ide's horseman who was now sawing with the bit at the poor creature in a cruel manner, so that he could turn again and perhaps jump the tumbril. He was a young man and fit, with the topknot and swords of a samurai and a dark face that might have been

---

34 A sort of crude wagon.

handsome had it not been distorted into such a mask of terror as I have never seen before. He was so pale with fright that his skin almost seemed to glow in the luminous rays of the moon.

"Ho, ho, my fine fellow, I shall have you and find out what has you in such a lather," I thought and burst out of the trees just as he was about to spur his horse for the jump. She screamed and reared, throwing him and bolting for cover. I ran over to the fallen man, ready to demand his surrender when much to my surprise he grabbed my wrist, planted his foot on my chest and with a shrill cry hurled me head over heels into the undergrowth. I landed heavily, knocking the wind from me for a second time in as many minutes. I lay there in stunned surprise until I heard a noise that convinced me that my man had regained his feet. I heaved myself up just in time for he narrowly missed my head with his sword. I dived to recover my own blade putting a tree between myself and my attacker. He was a tall man and obviously in an acute state of nervous tension for his face was utterly white and he trembled. He bared his teeth and his eyes widened when he saw me clearly for the first time.

I tried to address him in Japanese telling him that we didn't need to fight if he would just be a good fellow and put up his sword. He gave no reply to this, but only rushed at me screaming a ferocious battle cry. I took the blow on my guard and sent him several quick ripostes that drove him back. He swung wildly at me again and it became clear that he was attempting to cut a way to his horse somewhere behind me. I guarded again, confident now that this terrified boy's wild swings were no real threat and that if I was careful, I might disarm him with a cut to the hand. I dodged or slipped his next few strokes, maneuvering inside his guard when the cost of my arrogance came home to me. I came close to delivering the blow to the wrist when he grabbed me by the sleeve and dragged me close before delivering an unguentlemanly blow that left me gasping. I hobbled back furiously, fighting for my life against the flurry of cuts, until I tripped and fell flat on my back. My opponent, scenting victory, hurled himself forward, his blade held high in both hands to deliver a perfect killing stroke only to find himself impaled on my steel which I had thrust out ahead of me as I fell. His eyes were wide with shock and rage. As he slumped forward I rolled out from under him. He lay face down, my sword trapped beneath him, swinging at me weakly as he died, his arms thrashing like a drowning man. I kicked the sword from his grasp, my blade blossoming from his back. I pushed him over with my foot and he howled. A red foam was already at his mouth, the wound was mortal, hitting both bowels and lungs. He clawed at me and at the sword that stuck from his stomach, I pulled it out and he almost fainted, shrieking like a wounded horse. I steadied myself, still reeling from the low blow he had dealt me and knew that this could not go on. Thinking of poor Yoshi whose beheading had been botched by Lord Ide's men. I made the two handed hold that Otaro had taught me and brought it down in one swift stroke. I did not need another.

As I cleaned and sheathed my sword, I could hear Otaro and Jingen nearby and I limped back towards them. The dead man's horse had run and I could still hear her hoofbeats in the distance.

I had neither the energy nor the inclination to pursue. As I came around the bend, clambering over the tumbrel, I was greatly shocked to see Otaro limping up the road, bleeding profusely from a head wound and leading Rocinante, who was trembling with fright and utterly spent, carrying the body of Jingen slung across the saddle. I rushed forward as fast as my injury would allow.

"Where are the others? Are you badly hurt? Is poor Jingen killed?"

I moved quickly and had the reins before he could answer. He was gone, every atom of energy having been wrung from him. I half led, half carried him back to the house that we had left, Jingen was pale and still breathing, but Otaro was growing fainter and fainter. Jingen I laid on a mat. He seemed fine but for a livid bruise upon the temple that explained his insensible state. I was more concerned about Otaro, who was so fatigued that he could not speak and fell into a deep sleep as soon as I laid him down. I washed his wound and was much relieved to discover that it was but a torn scalp. A glancing blow had been turned by the thick hair of his topknot and had cut a flap of skin from the top of his head. I searched the houses until I found some sewing stuff and made the best job of it that I could. The scalp is a deal easier then many other cuts to sew and I do not feel that I made a bad job of it considering the circumstances. Sewing skin together by the light of a paper lantern is a tricky business.

The first light of dawn was beginning to break and there was still Rocinante to be thought of. I was much worried that she might have been ruined by neglect in the month of my absence, but in truth the situation was not as bad as might be. Jingen had ridden her hard and by the state of her stomach, he had been none too picky about her feed. Her mouth was cut from the bit, but that was new and most likely inflicted in the panic of the night before. On the other hand, she had been rested, unsaddled, and let to the halter. She'd also been rubbed down, however inexpertly, and those wounds she had taken in the battle by the falls, cuts and burns on her flanks, for the most part had been cleaned and tended to. For a mare abandoned to the vagaries of fate and an unschooled master she had not fared too badly.

Though I was greatly fatigued by the labours of the night, I was also heartened to have both Jingen and Rocinante, back hale and hearty, though curiosity was gnawing at me as to how Otaro had received his wound. I did not have much time to think on it as the quiet of the early morning was shattered by a horrifying series of howls and screams that echoed from where I had left Jingen. Leaving Rocinante, I rushed to his side, sword drawn, ready for anything convinced that he was being horribly murdered. My appearance did nothing to calm him and he screamed and screamed even more hysterically, his broad honest face so pale beneath its dirt that the bright purple bruise on his head stood out like the greasepaint of a clown.

"Ghosts, oh ghosts, please spare me, spare me master ghost, I was your friend and servant, mercy please, please have mercy."

He fell on his knees and grovelled before me, hammering his head off the ground in an obeisance that was as alien to my republican principles as his craven cries for mercy. Having established that he was not being murdered and was in fact, merely an unbalanced halfwit, I informed him in no uncertain terms that I was not a ghost, that I was his friend and would he please stop that degrading bowing, as offensive to a man of liberty as any insult, and would he like something to eat? My tirade took him quite aback and he lay there looking up at me with the air of a faithful hound, who does not know how he has done wrong. I repeated my question about the food, for though we had little enough store, the poor fellow looked half starved, and he nodded. I turned to retrieve the food bag and dole him out a ration, when he fell upon me from behind, seizing my leg and throwing me almost to the floor.

I had had quite enough of oriental wrestling tricks the night before and was about to stroke him with the butt of my blade when he wrenched off my left shoe with a cry of triumph and tore away my sock in almost the same movement. There was a yell of relief and exultation and I suddenly felt myself released, but not before horrible slobbering kisses had been planted all over my naked foot. I sprang to my feet, blushing furiously, sure that something terribly improper had occurred though not sure what. I drew myself up with as much dignity as a man can in one shoe and one sock, but was immediately overwhelmed by another series of bows from the humble Jingen, now vocal in joy rather than terror.

"Oh Captain, thank you, thank you, I was so sure you were dead and Mr. Otaro too, oh thank you, thank you, thank you for saving me from those terrible ghosts."

And so he continued in that vein until, at a loss at how to proceed, I retrieved my footwear and donning it again, directed him to where he could find food and ordered him to prepare a breakfast for the three of us.

I left him to it, while I sat on the porch and tried to wipe the worst of his saliva from my foot before replacing my sock and brogue. I stepped into the other room to find Otaro sitting up, woken by the clamor. He looked pale and wan. Scalp wounds are rarely serious, but they bleed profusely and Otaro at that time had no great reserves of strength. He sat with the blanket gathered about him and his hands folded across his rounded stomach, regarding me.

"He is whole and well, Captain, I am sorry that I had to strike him last night, I know you are fond of him, but he was in the way and they would have killed us both if I had not prevented him from panicking."

I sat down, burning with questions, but before I could begin, he had one of his own. "That fellow you chased after, Captain Robert, did he get away?"

"No"

"Oh, that is good"

"I had thought he was chasing Jingen, but he seemed more intent on fleeing himself."

"It was the men in white again, Captain, they were fleeing from the men in white. Two of Lord Ide's men had been tracking our guest, thinking him a scout for Lord Hoji probably, but they fell prey themselves to the men in white. One of them fell, I saw the body. It is not far from here."

"Was it one of the men in white that gave you that cut to the head?"

He nodded and touched it delicately. "Yes, but I struck him down before he could do any greater harm and took after his comrade who was attempting to slay our guest out there."

"How many were there?"

"Two that I could see"

"Are those their swords?"

"Yes"

"Are there any distinguishing marks on them?"

"Perhaps, though I'm sure Master Sum will be able to identify them for us. They are fine blades carried by skilled swordsmen. He will recognize the marks, I have not the skill."

I could have danced a jig right there and then, our first real clue as to the identity of these murderous assassins. After nearly five weeks of frustration, we finally had something that we could trace back to them. All we had to do was find the old fellow. He would work his magic and we would know who those white-clad "ghosts" were. And where they were, we would find the boy and the swords and the whole sanguinary business would be at an end. I stopped for a moment.

"Two you say, where did the third sword come from?"

"From the second rider. It would not do to leave it where it might be stolen. Great evil could be done with such a weapon in the wrong hands."

I did not argue, I had examined the lot when I'd unloaded Rocinante and the third blade had seemed of no great account. It was just another instance of Otaro being overly precious about swords, a common enough characteristic of samurai.

It was with this in mind that I consented somewhat sullenly to Otaro's suggestion that I should recover the sword left by the man I had slain. I was dog tired, but disinclined to argue when he seemed so sick and so, leaving him in Jingen's care (who had happily looted the vegetable gardens around us and was making soup). I marched off through my fatigue to the place where the man had fallen. My bones and body ached and I rubbed my hand where I had jarred it the night before, but all this was forgotten when I came upon the place. The marks of the previous night's fight were plain; the trampled leaves of the forest floor, the dark stain of blood not yet quite dry. But the body was gone, as were all his acoutrements, including that damned sword. I swore and looked around me, but I could not see any mark of the intruders passing. The men in white must have taken them. No wild animal was going to make off with a whole body or its weapons. But if they were so close, why did they not rush us or had they lost all stomach for the fight after Otaro had slain two of their number? I could understand why they would remove their own dead, to prevent discovery, but why take a stranger? Surely he would bring a searcher no closer to uncovering them. I gave it up as useless and, having satisfied myself that the man's horse was long gone and that no-one remained skulking around, I made my way back to camp. I returned to find Jingen presiding over a bubbling pot which excellent, while Otaro sat on the porch waiting. He seemed unsurprised that I had returned empty handed and the idea that he somehow knew I would infuriated me.

"He was gone." I said, "they must have taken him, though they left no sign of their doing so."

"I thought that they might."

"And yet you sent me anyway."

"My dear Captain Robert, I thought that they might do it. It was a supposition and you through your labour have turned it into a fact. As to why they did this, I have no idea, but consider this. They killed Lord Hoji and his guards, but they took no bodies and only took his swords, leaving all others." He indicated Jingen. "They killed this man's family and left their bodies also, but this fellow whom you killed, they took both body and sword. Why? I have no idea. Why would men who had been previously happy to leave the bodies of their victims on the field change now? I am in complete agreement with you that Lord Ide is innocent of involvement, so it is not to shield him. Also his men were fleeing from the white-clad men, what possible use could they have for the body of one of their slain enemies?"

This torrent of reasoning left me quite dumb, but convinced me that my journey had not been completely in vain. A reconnaissance that reveals the absence of the enemy can be quite as useful as one that finds him. There were any number of uses a freshly killed body could be put to, I mused, given the political situation between Lord Ide and Lord Hoji. But all of this was distracting from the fact that Jingen had produced some excellent victuals and was obviously keen to feed us. We ate and after the thin fare of the days before it was a feast, nourishing and hot, sticking to the ribs in a most agreeable manner. On seeing that we had had our fill and on refilling our cups with cool clear water from the village well, he himself ate and we sat for a while in a state of companionable digestion before questioning him.

I took the lead as Jingen had an affection for me that he did not have for Otaro, who had fastidiously served himself from a bowl that our humble cook had not touched when breakfast had been served. He interjected occasionally, mainly to correct me or suggest an alternate choice of word. Jingen's tale was a long and rambling one, with repeated asides regarding the sweetness and docility of my mare, who had bitten him only once, and such food as had been available to him as well as the state of health and regularity of his bowels, in whose earnest study he was much taken, a characteristic that forcibly reminded me of a late uncle of mine. But we got the story out of him in the end. He began by stating that he was happy that we were not dead, as he had thought when he had recovered on the battlefield by the falls to find us long gone. "Dead or ghosts," he added laughing and pointing at my feet at which point the reason for his bizarre attack some hours before became clear[35]. He explained that he had been living hand to mouth for the last month or so while we were in captivity, dodging Lord Hoji's and Lord Ide's patrols as well as the "ghosts" (the men in white), any one of whom would have killed him for being a traitor, or a loyal subject of Lord Ide's or simply on general principles.

The news was as follows, the devastation of the land had become quite general with Lord Hoji's men having the best of it. Lord Ide's peasants were huddling together in a few well defended villages and were refusing to harvest without armed guards. A deputation of merchants had been sent to Yeddo to beg the intercession of the Mikado, but they had been cut down by mysterious assailants. Lord Ide was dispatching a heavily armed escort with another embassy to explain his lateness in beginning his trip to the capital[36]. Word of the murder of Lord Hoji had leaked out, with most people blaming either the "ghosts" or Lord Ide. No one knew what to think, though there was talk that the pope himself would dispatch an investigator to discover the truth. Otaro who had been silent all this time, slapped his belly

---

35 You will remember that in Japanese mythology, ghosts have no feet.

36 Japanese noblemen were expected to stay in the capital for six months of the year, mainly so that they couldn't get up to mischief and so that the Shogun could keep an eye on them.

and laughed a good deal. Jingen looked rather sour at Otaro's laughter. Presumably like most Japanese, he thought very highly of the pope and said so, continuing that he hoped the pope's messenger arrived soon as Lord Hoji was leading an army to Lord Ide's castle and would most likely wipe him out.

This stopped Otaro's merriment quickly enough. The movement of armies is no laughing matter in a country as peaceful as Japan.

"Where is this army?" interrupted Otaro addressing Jingen directly for the first time.

"A days walk from here, not more my Lord," said Jingen dropping his head suddenly. Otaro looked at me very seriously, "We must go there at once, firstly to learn the news and second to talk him out of this madness."

I agreed and we gathered ourselves swiftly. I mounted Otaro on Rocinante despite his protests. I was tired and had not slept, but he had fought three opponents, had been starved and had taken a wound. I would not budge. And so with Jingen leading Rocinante and loaded down with what vegetables we could carry, we set out to turn back the army of Lord Hoji.

17

*We meet an army.
Lord Hoji proves not as mad as he appears.
Sad news.
I issue a challenge.*

It was a hard day's march. Otaro dozed as we plodded forward, Jingen leading the way, to Lord Hoji's encampment. That his decision to attack Lord Ide's castle was an act of lunacy was clear to me at least. He had no artillery and few guns, his main strength was in cavalry. And while Lord Ide's castle was hardly worthy of the name, it occupied an enviable position that made it impregnable to escalade[37] or to an infantry assault. To run cavalry across that little spit of land was crazy. Infantry will not break when they have nowhere to run to and while Lord Ide's riflemen were no samurai, they had proven they were men of mettle who could "fire and load like guardsmen". Not only that but in Major Fitzpatrick, Lord Ide had a proven leader of men with more experience of battle than any of Lord Hoji's samurai. Raiding villages is an entirely different proposition to facing a line of battle. Hoji's only hope, as far as I could see, was for Ide to give battle, in a place suited to cavalry and commit some blunder, perhaps refusing Major Fitzpatrick command. I pondered this

---

[37] Attacking an enemy fortress by literally climbing over the walls, usually using ladders.

question as we trudged on. I could see a village in the distance, the houses like a print, picturesque in the morning sunlight, the small shrine standing at the village entrance like a sentinel. The water in the paddies below gleamed like silver, undisturbed by the familiar lines of peasants at their work. The willow tree by the village pond was innocent of children. Greenery sprouted madly in a garden, tumbling over its enclosure in its haste to grow and a basket rocked on its side as the wind blew. The people had long since run from this place and the neatness of their daily industry was fading, prey to the elements and neglect.

The view was disheartening and I turned my face away, trying to find a man in the emptiness around us, some friendly dot to show that not all was strife, but there was none. Japan, while not exactly civilized, is thoroughly cultivated. The landscape shows everywhere the hand of man at work. It has none of the wilderness, the great forests or rushing rivers, of my own country, but it always has a sense of bustle and of work. I looked down the valley and felt thoroughly melancholic, this pretty country was far more deserted than ever the Great Plains could be. I shook myself to banish such gloomy thoughts.

Otaro was revived by the rest and seemed almost his old self again when we broke our march for lunch. Jingen cooked another fine stew and I napped, for I was badly fatigued. We pushed on afterwards and made good progress until we made camp in an abandoned village as darkness fell. Otaro took the first watch and Jingen the second so that I could get some rest and we pressed on hard in the morning, walking Rocinante to rest her until we crossed a ridgeline that led down the valley and found the whole of Lord Hoji's camp laid out before us.

There was a huge assemblage of people set out in an order that made no particular sense to me. Lord Hoji's tent was clear enough. It was large and marked by his banners, long streamers catching in the wind. Before it, there was a sort of ante-chamber of canvas open to the sky obviously a meeting place or parlour where the Lord would hold court. Around this were arranged the tents of his retainers and beyond that some crude shacks, no doubt for the servants and porters attached to the army. The horse lines were at least well situated, near, but not too near water and with forage[38] being cut and brought in. There were maybe five hundred men in all, not counting porters and servants, which was a sizeable force in these parts, and maybe a third of them mounted, which Lord Ide could not hope to match. What surprised me was that we had been challenged by not one picket[39] nor hailed by any sentinel. Had Major Fitzpatrick placed himself on this ridge, Lord Hoji's men would have had a very hot time of it. The other thing that I could not fathom was why the army was encamped here at all, as it was only a few days journey from one castle to the other, surely they could not have stopped for a rest? To be in camp at high noon made no sense at all. I was spared the burden of further speculation by the thump of approaching hooves as one of Lord Hoji's samurai spurred up to us from the camp.

---

38 By forage, Captain Hood means grass or straw gathered for the army's horses.
39 A line of sentries.

Otaro hailed him in a friendly fashion as we came closer and I recognized him as the gossipy fat man Yamagatu that Otaro had spoken of before. He greeted us warmly and said that we had been given up for dead. He and Otaro chatted as we slowly made our way back to the camp and soon there were heads poking out of tents and clusters of samurai loafing about trying not to gawk at the men who had come back from the grave. We were led through the maze of tents towards the open air parlour that I mentioned earlier. There we were greeted by old Ittei who was greatly discomfited by our appearance, not least our odour, and whose noble attempt at imperturbability was only slightly marred by the compulsive twitch of his nose when we were near. He steadied himself and after ordering old Yamagatu, who was grinning despite himself, to take Rocinante and Jingen to the horse lines. He disarmed us, placing our weapons on a black lacquered stand by the entrance to the audience chamber, guarded by two ferocious looking samurai sweating through the day in full battle armour. We were announced by Ittei and then entered. I must admit, I was gratified to hear the buzz of surprise that filled the chamber when our names were called out.

The chamber was the perfect picture of a samurai camp in the field. Lord Hoji sat on a small collapsible stool while his advisors sat around him on mats. They were immaculately dressed and their makeup was untroubled by any hint of dirt or perspiration. They were obviously engaged in a council of war, as there were maps and charts scattered between them, which one of the younger samurai gathered up as we entered. Lord Hoji's battle armour sat on a stand to one side and was almost knocked over when the young man surprised at our appearance, stepped back too far. Lord Hoji growled at him and became impassive as we advanced and made our bow.

"Greetings magistrate, we had heard that you had been killed by Lord Ide's men, I am glad to see that it is not so."

"Thank you Lord," said Otaro, bowing again, "our lives were spared by the vagaries of fate and we were taken prisoner. I was only delivered by the courageous actions of my friend here, Captain Robert Hood, who rescued me from a most ignominious end at the treacherous hands of Lord Ide." I bowed when I was referred to, mainly to hide my blushes. I did not care to see Otaro belittle himself before these oafs, but I supposed he knew what he was doing.

"That is well," said Lord Hoji and listened patiently enough when Otaro gave an abbreviated account of our adventures. He would occasionally interrupt with more questions, none of which I noticed had anything to do with the purpose of our mission, finding the murderers of his uncle and rescuing his kidnapped cousin. Only at one point was I called upon to speak. I had drifted off after having failed to spot either Master Sum, Kaneda or old Hiramatsu amongst the samurai at Lord Hoji's side and so, had to have Otaro repeat Lord Hoji's question before I could respond.

"These rifles, Captain, how many does Lord Ide have. Where did they come from and how good are his men at shooting with them?"

Otaro gave me a fierce look, embarrassed at having to repeat the question.

"He has about two hundred," I replied. "They are from England where they make fine rifles. He has men for all of them, but perhaps only eighty that are really skilled in their use".

I did not add that those eighty men were the personal command of Major Fitzpatrick and that the men under the gallant hats were likely to break and run given the opportunity. I doubted Lord Hoji would appreciate any denigration of Japanese arms, even those of an enemy.

"And is England near America?"

I coughed to hide my amusement.

"No, though we were once ruled by their king. We revolted when he became vile and tyrannous. There is a vast ocean between us, though we do speak the same language and have a great deal in common."

"So you are enemies then."

"Not exactly." I thought back to the Oregon question and the high handedness of the British. "But we are not exactly friends either".

I was in the middle of adding that cousins squabble when Otaro, who was withholding his impatience with difficulty, cut in and began "Lord, I commend you for your zeal in acting against Lord Ide, who has most treacherously flouted the laws of the land by trafficking with foreigners and making allies of foreign powers without recourse to the Tycoon. However, it is vital, if your vigorous action is to be rewarded, that a messenger be dispatched to Yeddo immediately so that the government can learn the full extent of his crimes. I implore you to put such a courier at my disposal. Forces from Yeddo will take time to get here and cannot possibly arrive in time to rob you of the glory of crushing him, but they should be here so that you gain the rightful credit of your actions."

It was a masterful stroke and silenced Lord Hoji's objections before he voiced them. He could not but agree. Here was Otaro offering to put his weight behind his ludicrous war if only he would let him and offering to speak for him in the capital. There were some distrustful looks from the advisors of course, but since no-one could think of a reasonable objection, the point was made. Otaro, begged pen and paper so that he might write his report then and there, and a courier was summoned and dispatched with all haste for Yeddo. We were then dismissed and passed to the hands of Ittei again who seemed only too happy to oblige us with a bath.

It is only those who have been on campaign who have an idea of what it is to be truly clean, to experience the pink-skinned feeling of being completely reborn, that soap and water brings after several weeks of their absence. You walk taller, your voice takes on a deeper and more manly tone and your whole being is cleansed. Whatever may be said about the barbarity of Japanese culture in some respects, they are a people who understand and value cleanliness and have raised the act of bathing from a necessity to a pleasure. Porters brought us tubs of icy cold water from the river and we scrubbed with cloth and soap until we were quite raw. I had not bathed with Otaro before and was a little taken aback by the frank curiosity with which he regarded my body, until I realized that he was making a study of the various scars and marks that have been left there by musket ball, lance, sabre, tomahawk and pistol bullet. He had a few himself, sword cuts in the main and we swapped stories of this or that wound while the porters brought small streaming tubs of water into which we lowered ourselves. That is the way of it in Japan, you clean yourself first and then bathe, we sat there hunched up in our deliciously hot tubs of almost boiling water for nearly an hour until we emerged red as two lobsters, but most refreshed. Jingen because of his humble origins was not afforded the same facilities, though soap and water were made available and to our surprise and delight he made good use of them, returning with the news that Rocinante was being taken care of and looking as if he'd been skinned. More than anything the wash lifted our spirits and after an excellent meal and a nap, we were in fine shape again.

I went to check on Rocinante and saw the oriental grooms had done as well as oriental grooms can. Otaro went in search of Master Sum with the captured swords slung over his shoulder as a railsplitter[40] totes his axe on his way home from work. Old Yamagatu accompanied me at Otaro's request as Europeans were none too popular with samurai who had so lately tasted

---

40 A sort of American labourer who makes fences from crudely cut logs stacked on top of each other. Abraham Lincoln was perhaps the most famous example and was so fond of the work that he kept an axe and several logs close at hand in the White House for when he needed to do some serious thinking.

defeat at the hands of rifle wielding heralds of progress with a white man at their head. Yamagatu was a short fat little man, whose luxurious moustache covered the worst of the hare lip that marred his face. He was genial company and we talked a great deal on our way to and from the horse lines. He told me that nothing further had been learned about the murder or the kidnapping and the reports of the white-clad swordsmen were dismissed as peasant fairytales. He did answer a question that had puzzled me a great deal. By the lines there was a large pond fed by a small stream around which scaffolding was being build. Divers bobbed up and down in the pond, while dripping engineers called to each other as a great tripod was being erected.

"You see", said Yamagatu, "back in the old days, there were a lot of wars in these parts, but eventually a stop was put to it and all the guns were destroyed or lost." I had a sudden idea of what he was about. "Or hidden?"

"Indeed, the cannon were sunk in this pond probably so that the priest couldn't turn them into temple bells or something. Anyway you'd be mad to attack a castle without artillery, so here friend, is our artillery."

There was a sound of rushing water and a cheer from the porters who were hauling on the ropes in teams. What I had assumed was a scaffolding in the process of construction was in fact a hoist in use. A small man erupted from the water, balancing himself on the barrel of a cannon around which had been slung several ropes. Water gushed from the mouth of the gun as it shifted under his weight, the verdigrised muzzle splashing the crews on the ropes as it, was swung onto dry land, where it was immediately seized and dragged away.

Perhaps Lord Hoji was not as crazy or stupid as I had supposed. We were making our way back to the tent where Otaro had said he would meet us, when my hand fell on my sword, and I felt the sudden impulse to find and thank Hiramatsu for his kindness , which had been so instrumental in saving our lives. I asked Yamagatu where the old man was to be found. Yamagatu's fat face darkened and he said the Hiramatsu was not with the company.

"Where is he then? I can't imagine that the old man would miss this for the world. Is he ill?"

My companion turned away and tried to talk of other things, but he had not Otaro's gift of leading me away from topics he did not wish to discuss and I pressed the point.

"He is dead Captain, killed in a duel," he said finally when I would give him no peace. "It was a bad business and it is best not to speak of it."

"Who killed him?" I demanded growing more heated by the moment. "What was the cause of the duel? He was an old man, what was he doing fighting one at all?"

Yamagatu could not meet my eye.

"Kaneda killed him. There was talk of an insult, that he had said Hiramatsu had dishonoured his son's memory by passing his sword to a foreigner and that in doing so had shamed us all.

Hiramatsu went to him to find the truth and was offered such scorn that he had to challenge him. It was quick. He wanted to die really. There was only one cut. Kaneda may be a bad man, but he is a good swordsman."

I listened to this with growing incredulity and a coldness in my heart. Our jovial drunken host was dead, slain by the man who had sworn he would kill me, but who on finding me beyond his reach had turned on a man who was within his power. Hiramatsu's only crime was to have made an ill considered gift to me who barely understood what I had been given. I had caused his death by not facing Kaneda when I had the chance.

"What did Lord Hoji say to this?"

Yamagatu cut in "It was a dispute between men and Kaneda is one of the Lord's favourites. He could not expect him to turn down a challenge."

And with that my rage blossomed, my limbs trembled and my heart beat faster and faster as my fury coursed hot and cold through me. I felt my lips pulling back into a grimace and I bared my teeth. I ran about the camp, Yamagatu hard on my heels shouting, but I could not hear him. I charged through crowds of glistening divers and lounging samurai until I spied Kaneda by the door of Lord Hoji's audience chamber. His tall thin form was turned away from me, though as he spoke to one of his fellows, he saw me and what I believed was a smirk crossed his pale features. My eyes narrowed and I could feel the blood pounding in my ears, drowning our Yamagatu's appeals to reason.

"You," I cried pointing at him "you murderous – and I uttered a curse, come here and fight me like a man."

He smiled delicately, his white makeup and carefully applied rouge was perfect, which infuriated me all the more. His tone was cool and imperious, "Have a care foreigner, I do not fight hairy children who cannot control their tempers."

His friends tittered at this and I grew even more enraged. "Yes, do have a care. Strange person. Though my Lord is indulgent of you, I am not as generous or as wise as he and might have to slay you if you continue, as I have found it necessary to do on occasion with people who do not know their place."

He turned and began to walk away, his friends congratulating him and with the sing-song laughter ringing in my ears I went for him. I saw Otaro's face wide with astonishment over Kaneda's shoulder as I rushed towards him. I felt Yamagatu's hand on my back as vainly tried to keep me.

And then I had him, grabbing his swords and twisting them I pushed him, steering him by the collar of his robe, as a man would push a wheelbarrow, barreling through his flock of admirers as he scrambled on all fours to save his face from the dust until I ran him right into a tent post, kicking him in the seat of the pants all the while.

"Oh you will not fight me, will you not? Wish to spare me do you? You rotten little coward."

He sprang up and I knocked him down again and he scuttled backwards on his hands trying to dodge the kicks I aimed at him. His robe was twisted about exposing his bare legs and stomach. He had lost his swords and his face paint was dirty and the red lip smudged so that he looked more like a drunken Irish doxy than the reserved samurai of old. I stood over him about to unleash another fusillade of abuse, when two of Lord Hoji's guard ran up rattling in their armour and with their hands at their weapons. Their Lord followed them at a decent interval, by which time Kaneda had picked himself off the ground and was setting himself to rights. He began before I had even registered Lord Hoji's presence.

"Lord, this animal is mad, he has attacked me without cause and must be punished."

He was about to continue, when I turned and saw Lord Hoji raise his hand even as Kaneda's lackeys began to babble in noisy agreement. Otaro was standing by him, still carrying his bushel of swords and panting heavily. He looked as if he was about to speak when Lord Hoji pre-empted him. "Must, Kaneda? Must? I shall see about that, only I decide what must or must not be done." Kaneda shrank from the rebuke.

"What say you foreigner, did you attack him?"

I bowed, "I did, Lord, for he refused a challenge." The nobleman paused for a moment and regarded Kaneda critically, but not without the hint of a smile.

"That is not like you, Kaneda. You are usually so quick to take offence"

"But Lord this man is a barbarian, to fight him would bring no…"

I interrupted him and was rewarded with a savage look, "with the Lord's permission, I will continue until sufficient insult has been offered." The shadow of the smile on his face deepened and he turned to Otaro, who had put down his burden and was watching me with the same impassive aspect that was always his custom.

"Tell me magistrate, is your friend capable of issuing a challenge, is he a man of rank?"

"He is, Lord," said Otaro without hesitation, "and well aware of the consequences."

"Well then, Kaneda," said Lord Hoji to the outraged man who was now trembling with fury, "you must take up the challenge or suffer constant insult, it seems."

"Then I take it up Lord," he said looking daggers at me, "with pleasure".

Lord Hoji thought a moment and then said, "Tomorrow morning will be soon enough, there is the business of the guns to be settled first and I will not have the men distracted. Just after dawn, I think, as I do not wish to lose too much of the light, but it will not take long." And so it was done. Kaneda was hustled away by his friends and Otaro and Yamagatu took me by the arms and led me to Yamagatu's tent where we were being lodged.

"Well, Captain, life is certainly not without incident with you around. You learned of Hiramatsu's death I see. It was not a bad one, he was courageous to the last, but I had hoped you would not learn of it until we were away again. It complicates things, I suppose, but it was fated and is therefore inescapable."

I suddenly became quite embarrassed having not realized how my actions might have compromised our mission, to apologise would be fatuous, so I stumbled for something to say.

"So what did Master Sum have to say about the swords, who do they belong to?"

"Ah, so you remember our purpose here, Captain," and I flushed again. "He had very little to say as he is not here. He retired to his house by the lakeside some time ago and hasn't been seen since, so it looks like we will have to pay a call on him anyway."

18

The duel.

We slept as best we could. Otaro was the very model of calm and Yamagatu was a genial host, so that the day was spent companionably. We watched the engineering work by the pond. Lord Hoji's men were busy scraping and cleaning the bronze cannon they had recovered, while others worked at a portable forge to cast shot and fittings for the new carriages. They hammered through the night, working by torch light so that by the next morning they had three carriages and could expect to have a small store of balls within a day or two. I spent the night in quiet contemplation of what I had done and wrote two letters for my people. Otaro was to get them to Francis Hall if the worst happened. What I was engaged in was no great Christian thing, but I cannot believe that my Lord would judge me alright if I were to let a murderer and a bully make free with the lives of those who had been kind to me. A Christian must also be a man of honour, if he is to hold his head up high before his God. This may be just my explaining away of my own sinful nature, but I have always taken great comfort from the words of thirteenth

Romans, "But if you do evil, be afraid; for he does not bear the sword in vain."

Otaro fussed over me a great deal that night and made sure that my clothes were washed and dry in time for the morrow. I had shucked my dirty clothes on bathing and had been wearing a robe ever since. It did not suit me much, since I was much taller than the previous owner. But thanks to Otaro's good offices I went to the field in linen, that while worn, was clean. He also answered my few questions regarding etiquette, seconds and the like. "Oh no, it's very simple, he will kill you or you will kill him. We will all come and watch of course. Duels are quite rare these days, you see. You should watch him though. He is pure Yakamaru and very fast. There will be one strike, it will be lethal, or not, but if you survive you should have him. But most importantly be aware of the length of his blade. He has perhaps an inch or two on you there and he is clever and probably knows it. He will let you strike first, probably, trusting to the slightly shorter length of your sword to save him, then strike you with the tip of his own. I would not presume to advise you, Captain Robert, you who have been in many more battles than I, but I would say that it would be best for you to fight him in the middle distance. Too far away and he holds the advantage by virtue of the superior length of his blade, too close and he will use wrestling against you in which you are unschooled. I leave it to your judgement."

His concern was affecting and his advice useful, though it was a matter that I had given great thought to over the last few hours and I had already formulated my plan of campaign.

It was a bright morning and the early sunlight was clear and cool, so that the grasses and the whole world seemed reborn, still wet with dew and full of promise as we walked to the field. There were a dozen of us, Otaro and Yamagatu acting for me and a gaggle of painted courtiers acting for Kaneda, the man himself having dressed entirely in white for the occasion, presumably to show that he was prepared for death or some such nonsense. I glanced quizzically at Otaro when I saw Kaneda's outfit, but he shook his head. It was just another affectation.

Kaneda paused before the field and one of his friends laid a sheet of paper and a brush before him, whereupon he knelt, scribbled something on the paper, yelling in a most peculiar way while he did so. He then washed his hands in a bowl of water, dried them with a towel handed to him by one of his lackeys and began to embark on such a series of ceremonies and other balderdash that I grew quite bored. I could see a line of people watching us from the camp, Lord Hoji amongst them. Otaro had told me that it had been decreed that the duel was a private matter, but it was a good crowd nonetheless. I removed my coat and hung it on a nearby tree while Kaneda's second screamed out a list of the man's antecedents, which went on a bit. Otaro responded with "Captain Robert Hood of the United States Dragoons, son of" and he paused " Mr and Mrs Hood of Boston, the United States American", which made me smile. And so to business, we drew sword and advanced on one another, until ordered to stop by the umpire. We took up positions and bowed and then waited for the umpire (Yamagatu doing double duty) to give the word which he did.

Kaneda slipped into the characteristic two handed grip of the samurai, eyeing me steadily, while I turned myself to the side, put my arm at my back and extended my sword arm, turning the edge upwards, my wrist easing to take the strain. He seemed puzzled by this, not having seen this grip before, but then settled down to wait for my attack. His eyes bored into me, watching me closely, his gaze on my shoulders waiting for me to show my move before I made it. I, of course, did the same, but I was pleased to note that his eyes wandered occasionally only to be snapped back when he caught himself. I had not attacked, which rattled him. He had expected a bull's rush after the events of the day before. A fly buzzed and one of the seconds coughed, and there was a growing murmuring from the camp. Kaneda was not whipping the barbarian as quickly as they had expected. I hoped that Lord Hoji had no pressing business that morning because the sun was over the horizon now and still neither of us had moved. Kaneda was fairly glowing with perspiration, his pasty white face beading with great shining drops of sweat that trickled down his face, cutting rivulets down the white cake of his makeup. I held myself as taut and steady as I could, but let the tip of my sword waver just a little. It was the first movement either of us had made and his eyes followed it without thinking. One of his seconds remarked on it in a whisper and was harangued by Yamagatu to keep his trap shut. Otaro joined him in telling the boy he was a disgrace. I could hear the anxiety in his voice. He knew I was tiring and was suddenly afraid for me. I knew he was thinking that it was a poor stance for a long duel and that I had been hard pressed these last few days. I was using an unfamiliar weapon and was overwrought by the death of my benefactor Hiramatsu. In my anger I had bitten off more than I could chew. And now this brightly painted young killer was going to kill me and there was nothing he could do.

The tip of my blade wandered again, more wildly now and I winced, shifting my arm. Kaneda licked his red rouged lips and tightened his grip. The murmuring was growing louder now, but I did not really hear it. There were catcalls from a world away. The sun was warm on my face and a cool breeze rustled the grasses. I could hear the panting and neighing of the horses as they took their morning feed. I wondered which one of them was Rocinante. My wrist trembled badly now. Five, maybe six minutes had passed and my guard was unsteady until I dropped it , turning my face to wipe the sweat from my eyes. In a duel at home, he would have stood off, waited for me to finish, but he obviously cared as little for my etiquette as I did for his. He was upon me in an instant, hurling his body forward, his sword coming down in a single scything strike that would have cut me in twain had I not stepped to one side and grabbing his hilt with my left hand, hammering my right into his face, bursting his nose as I did so. He struggled with the hold until I gripped one of his fingers in my left hand and bent it back savagely. It snapped with a crunch. He dropped his weapon and grasping his white robe, I brought a knee into his stomach that dropped him to the ground. He fell with a sob, blinded by the pain as I stepped around him and stamped hard on his right ankle, repeating the step until it was crushed beneath my foot. He shrieked like a gelded thing, his mouth a yawning maw of blood and pain, until taking his samurai topknot in my hand I sawed it off with Hiramatsu's gift and then plunged him face first into the long grass with my boot at his back. The duel was over.

A low groan came to us on the wind as I walked towards Otaro, who had collected my coat. The line of men on the ridge were turning away, while Kaneda's seconds stared at us open mouthed, stunned into silence even as their man lay writhing on the ground.

"You should kill him, it would be merciful," said Otaro, who taking the severed topknot I handed him tossed it away and helped me on with my coat.

"I am not inclined to mercy today," I said fierce with barely satiated rage. "Anyway, I have killed him as surely as if I had stabbed him through the heart." And if what Otaro and Major Fitzpatrick had told me of the samurai honour code was true, I had. I doubt he would be able to cut his own belly with a hand with a broken finger and the pain of a smashed ankle, but one of his seconds would behead him before he could utter another cry to disgrace himself and if they did not, it was no concern of mine.

Otaro and I walked back to the camp, where men loudly went about their business as if none of them had been watching.

"Well, I am glad I asked Lord Hoji for a second horse before that little display. He will not be happy, but he gave the horse gladly thinking you would have no need of it. But tell me, Captain, how did you know he would attack when you weakened?"

"I didn't, but I thought he would."

"Is that why you took up that ridiculous stance? So that he would act knowing that you were weakened?"

"I wasn't weakened. Any man who must hold a sabre at the charge for half an hour on drill could handle as light a thing as Hiramatsu's sword in the same manner until the cows came home."

"So the weakening was a ruse then?"

"Yes, Otaro, a ruse." I said becoming tetchy as we reached the camp. Men were studiously avoiding our gaze. I was about to remonstrate with him on his crack about a ridiculous stance, when he interrupted me, casting a look over his shoulder.

"Ah, there. It is done. I wonder if he cried out. Well, it is of no matter. Shall we get the horses?"

19

*Stories of spirits.
Master Sum's house.*

It seemed that we were so unwelcome in Lord Hoji's camp that we were on the road again, within minutes. I was back on the ever faithful Rocinante and Otaro was atop a timorous bay gelding who was to prove as balky a horse as ever I came across. We moved on up the valley side, moving westwards, Jingen leading the way as he claimed he knew Master Sum's retreat. I didn't really believe him, but supposed that between our directions and Jingen's local knowledge, we could not go far wrong. I had had justice for my dead friend and in doing so escaped death myself, so nothing was likely to spoil my mood, which was as good as could be. Otaro interviewed me at length as to my strategy in the duel, which fascinated him in a purely professional sense and even Jingen congratulated me with a broad grin and a downwards chopping motion before telling me that I was lucky and blessed by a guardian spirit. This jovial blasphemy amused me and I would have questioned him as to what he meant had not Otaro suddenly interrupted the conversation with a harsh rebuke for Jingen, who looked crestfallen when he was told that guardian spirits were a baseless superstition and not to be entertained by a modern man. This was nonsense as Jingen was in no way a modern man and as entitled to his superstitions, within reason, as the backwoods yankee is at home entitled to distrust black cats or look askance at the call of the whipor wills[41]. I was not inclined to push the matter and we rode on in companionable silence, making it into the high valleys that day and making camp in the firm belief that we would reach Master Sum's the next day.

It was a quiet night and Otaro took first watch, as I was doing all I could to spare his strength. The cut to his head was pink and healthy, but I did not want to try him too hard if it wasn't necessary. Anyway it afforded me a chance to talk to Jingen unobserved and when I woke him to take the last watch, I stayed up for a few minutes to ask him about the guardian spirits that he had spoken of. It was a lengthy interview as I had not anticipated that Jingen lived in such a world of spirits, goblins, ogres and superstitions. It was a subject in which he was well versed and that held limitless interest for him. He held forth on the frog goblins who prey on travellers, but whose heads are shaped like pots and who can be overpowered only if you can trip them over and spill the water out. He spoke of the Kee-rin or the Japanese unicorn, that brings great good fortune and likes sweets. He also mentioned wise old crows, or was it ravens? These lived at the tops of mountains and instructed men in fencing, which is why he reckoned Master Sum lived on top of a mountain. He seemed to think Master Sum had one as a teacher, if he wasn't one in

---

[41] A type of small nesting bird, common in New England, whose call is thought to be an ill omen.

disguise himself. He told me quite seriously that I had been wise not to kill Kaneda because if I had, his vengeful ghost would have come back to haunt me.

"Then you have to get a priest, Captain, and priest very expensive, even for Lord, better that he kill himself, that way when he die, he concentrate on not screaming rather then on haunting you and everyone knows that the dead can only perform their last wish in life."

Lucky for me indeed, I thought with a smile. For all his humble station in life and his job as a tanner and a charcoal burner. I never saw him once express dissatisfaction or ill feeling about his caste. He mourned his family, but was simply happy to be alive and fed. While he was certainly no stoic, he did not howl at the injustices of life too much and I have often thought of him in later years when things seemed grim.

"But, Jingen, you said that I have a guardian?" I said. humouring him, though it made me smile to think that he saw spirits and ghosts in what was simply the hand of providence. "Oh yes, Lord, great guardian who brings you luck, I can see even though the ghostees scared all the spirits out of the woods, yours is still with you. They chased her, but she always comes back."

"Really?"

"Oh yes, she likes you very much, the ghostees cannot get you," and he paused for a moment and there was a look of sadness on his face and perhaps the beginning of a tear and remembered suddenly who, guardian spirit or no, the ghostees did get. I spoke quickly to allow him no time for maudlin reflection. "So what is this guardian spirit, does she have a name?" Is she tall or short? Fat or thin? Pleasing or homely?"

Jingen started at this and gave such a sudden boisterous laugh that I feared he would wake Otaro.

"No, no, no Captain, Lord, she is very pretty, she is foxwife[42] you see, with many tails and magic in her toes."

"Oh really."

"Oh yes Lord, very pretty, you might marry her if you want, she make good wife, but can never take off ring."

He proceeded to tell me legions of things about foxes, who could change into beautiful girls, did magic and were very cunning if troublesome mates. There was no end to their ingenuity and guile; fox wife, fox nonsense. Otaro, you devious old heathen, I thought, no wonder you made light of it, for what foreigner could possibly be a bad fellow if one of the spirits of the land vouched for him. The unusual kindness and courtesy extended to me, even though I was "hairy barbarian", Jingen's trust, Hiramatsu's kindness, Lady Hoji's favour, it all became clear to me now. It had been a masterstroke, a stamp of approval more significant than a passport issued by the Mikado himself for he was a man, while a spirit was, well, a spirit, and beyond reproach or doubt. But it was getting on and it would be dawn in a few short hours, so I bade Jingen good night, and still chuckling at my friend's oriental cunning. I fell asleep thinking that there

---

[42] A Japanese mythological character, a vixen that can take the shape of a beautiful woman, often pictured with nine tails. A benevolent figures usually, they bring good luck and are well disposed towards children.

were more things on heaven and earth than were dreamt of in my philosophy.

We reached Master Sum's house the following morning, which was another beautiful day, the sort to make a man wish for a fishing pole and a quiet sleepy river to watch it by. We saw the house some distance away up the valley and Otaro cursed himself loudly for a fool for the round-about way we had come. It seemed that we had taken a quite circuitous route and that Lord Hoji's castle was only across the crest of the mountain. He had not realized it. I have a poor enough head for directions anyway, a criminal failing in an officer, which I have worked hard to overcome, but in this case I took his word for it. I had a sense of where we were, but Japanese maps are beyond me and I trusted his judgment. But we had arrived at last and that, so far as I was concerned was enough.

Still I had planned to make some fun of him that day by stopping to examine animal tracks and by making myself the cryptic comments of which he was so inordinately fond, but he looked at me so oddly the first time that I did it, that I thought it a poor joke and decided to leave it until he was in better humour. Since he had kept me in the dark for so long about my "guardian spirit", whom I wasn't sure he hadn't invented himself to ease my way, I felt he could take some ribbing on the subject in his turn. The fencing master's house was at the bottom of the peak, just behind a saddle that crossed the valley. It lay in the sort of shallow bowl formed thereby. There was a large still lake of shining water before the two low buildings that made up the master's establishment and between the lake and the houses there was a beach of bright white sand and pebbles, which obviously served the old man as a drilling ground I could see the posts and markers scattered about it.

I have always found it extraordinary that mankind always returns to the same few simple solutions to eternal problems. Master Sum's instruction posts would have been very familiar to my sabre master at West Point or indeed to the legionnaires of Vegetius[43]. When we were still some distance away, my eye was drawn to a movement at the rear of the house. I leaned over Rocinante's neck and saw a woman running out, dressed in the plain blue of a servant. I spurred forward and Otaro made after me as best he could, cursing his horse loudly. But she had scrambled through the brush, over the kitchen garden and was well into the trees before we drew rein by the house. The woman, whom I had not seen clearly, had seemed in such a state of agitation, that I could only assume that she was fleeing some sort of attack. But when we reached the place it was deathly still. There were no signs of a struggle, all was neat and quiet and as orderly as could be.

Otaro dismounted, while I made for the rear of the place to see if I could find any trace of her, but it was to no purpose. There was a broad expanse of rock that had been screened from our view by the garden. This would conceal her tracks until she entered the forest and to pursue her across it on horseback would simply to have invited injury. A job best left to Otaro's

---

[43] A 4th century Roman general and authority on military matters. He wrote that, "Neither the arena or the field of battle ever proved a man invincible in arms, except that those who were carefully taught training at the stake."

superior tracking skills, I thought. I returned to the front of the house, hallooing as I did so, to discover that Jingen had caught up and was holding Otaro's horse and watching my friend with a bemused expression. Otaro lay on all fours on the beach before the house, moving like a crab from point to point, but always with his nose pressed almost against the sand. I was as befuddled as Jingen until I realized that the sand bore the impressions, faint though they were and almost washed away by the recent rains, but still barely visible, of dozens of foot marks.

I began to speak, but Otaro raised his hand impatiently and I turned away rather than endure another snub. Jingen met my eye and shrugged, so I went and explored the house. It was small, with only five rooms, which was rather Spartan for a man of Master Sum's rank and skills. The living and sleeping arrangements were simple and only for Master Sum and a servant. There were tubs for bathing outside and a well stocked larder, though in truth the only part of the domestic arrangement that surprised me was the small library, mostly of Japanese texts, but also some in what I believed to be Dutch, and also the armoury. When I say armoury, it was really an indoor training room, to be used when inclement weather made practice on the beach impractical, and it was a fine one, being the largest room in the house. What was surprising was the sheer profusion of weapons. There were; pikes and axes, wooden training swords, staves, chains with wicked blades attached and curious three tined forks all in a row, but mostly swords. There were racks of them, lining the floor, of every conceivable type, shape and colour. There were large two handed weapons in the manner of a medieval broadsword, a variety of straight and curved blades, which may have been Chinese, and upwards of a dozen of the "long and the short" swords that are the badge of the samurai class. Even then I realized I was seeing the armoury in a depleted state, for several racks were empty. I was looking for signs of foul play and why the woman had fled, but there were none, at the time. I sat on the porch, putting on my shoes and watching Otaro as he continued to nose around in the dirt. I turned the thing over in my mind. I was thinking that I would have made straight after the woman, but he was the lawman and I should trust to his judgment, though why he should choose to grovel on the ground rather than pursue a living witness who might explain Master Sum's absence I could not understand. That was when it came to me and I was up and running towards him, yelling "Nine!" and almost tripping over my still unfamiliar sword belt.

Otaro's horse started at my cry and Jingen was struggling with it, when Otaro looked up at me with a look of intense irritation on his normally impassive face, the front of his robe marked with a perfect circle of sand where his stomach strained his belt. He wiped sand from his fingers as he rose to greet me.

"Captain Robert, calm yourself, I believe..." he began, but I cut him off and grabbing him by the sleeve dragged him protesting into the house, without so much as removing our shoes, and thrust him into the armoury. He staggered and looked about him, surprised no doubt, by the profusion of the weapons around him.

"Captain Robert, I..."

"Lord Hoji's murderers were skilled swordsmen, yes?"

"Captain Robert, there is…"

"There were skilled swordsmen, were they or were they not?"

"They were."

"Swordsmen of real talent, trained by a master and they were twelve in number, correct?"

"Correct, Captain, I really…"

"Here we stand Otaro in the house of the finest fencing master in these parts and we are in his training room and here we find," I grabbed them up as I counted, "one, two, three, four, five, six, seven, eight, and nine," and dashed them at his feet for emphasis, "stands of arms lying empty. Does this strike you as a coincidence?"

I stopped, breathing hard from the violence of emotion of having finally solved the riddle. Otaro smiled and straightened his kimono,

"Well done Captain, but you will admit, it could be a coincidence."

I began to argue, but he carried on, "Master Sum is not the only fencing master in these parts. There may be others. You never made the acquaintance of Lord Ide's instructor, but I presume he has one. I have been a teacher in my time and you do not accuse me."

I grew quite flushed and angry at this. Otaro seemed to me to be being more than usually contrary.

"But you must…" "Also, the missing weapons, they could be racks that have yet to be filled, Master Sum is obviously a collector, though how he managed to amass such a collection is beyond me. Swords do not come cheap."

In my state of irritation, this seemed such a minor point that it hardly seemed worthy considering. I was growing quite red in the face at this point and when Otaro began to lecture me in that infuriatingly calm school-masterish tone of his, I thought my blood was going to boil.

"The first case that he is a fencing master, could be coincidence, true?"

"True," I granted through gritted teeth.

"The second case that there are perhaps a suspicious number of weapons missing from his house, is less likely, but could also be a coincidence, could it not?"

"It could," I admitted with bad grace.

Otaro put his arm around me and we walked to the porch, he conciliatory, I downhearted when we paused and he indicated the beach with a wave of his hand.

"But that a man who is a fencing master and who has nine weapons missing from his house, also has seven students whom he drills on the beach, three of whom are Takeda, three of whom are from Satsuma, and one of whom definitely trained in Edo under Master Itcho, this I think is one coincidence too many," he said with an impish grin. "We have him, Captain Robert, we have him."

I turned on him then, punching him in the shoulder and calling him a cantankerous show-boating old so and so, while all the while I wrung his hand and we both grinned like men fit to burst. Jingen joined in the laughter, though I doubt if he understood the cause.

"So, we need to run him to ground" I said. "He obviously has the boy. He will soon enough know that we've been here. Where will he run to?"

"I don't know, but I think his servant knows and will lead us to him. But I am not sure however that he has the boy, or the swords for that matter."

"Why not?"

"If as I suspect, he was after the swords rather than the child, he would have left him on the ledge to die. Also if he had what he was looking for, why attack us? We discovered the bodies. We had the greatest opportunity to make away with the swords. Why else would he tell you a story about Labour's Reward, if not to gauge your reaction and see if you might not give yourself away?"

"So who does have the swords and the child then?"

"I don't know, Captain, but if he thinks we have the sword and he knows who has the child, we may be able to bargain that information out of him."

"And then hang him as a damned murderous kidnapper and any other of that mob that we can find."

"Yes, Captain, something like that."

20

*A fruitless search.
An equally fruitless argument and an extraordinary lady.*

We set off after the fleeing servant with a light heart. Having struggled with the problem for the best part of two months and finally to have at least a great part of it laid before us almost made me sing with the joy of it. We trailed around the forest, while Otaro studied the ground like a queer sort of oriental Hawkeye from "The Last of the Mohicans". I merely held the horses and followed. On the frontier we generally used native scouts for the work and while I was never any great reader of tracks, I like to think I was a better reader of men than most. There are Indians who will deal square with you and those who'll prevaricate and grow sulky and sullen on trading post liquor and being able to tell one from the other stood me in good stead as a young officer.

Be that as it may, the tracking was a slow business and we made little progress, though curiously the course led us backwards towards Lord Hoji's castle. It was painstaking work and Otaro was much put out by it, having to stop every few minutes when he had lost the trail. As the day wore on and the shadows began to lengthen, our spirits lowered somewhat and it seemed that

Otaro's decision to let the maid run and not pursue her directly was a poor one, though I kept that thought to myself for fear of aggravating him further. Still as we pushed through the thicker parts of the forest, my doubts on this and several other points began to grow and I felt it would be disloyal of me to keep them from him any longer. We had paused near a brook that trickled down the mountain side and Jingen was busy boiling rice for the midday meal. His earnest attitude and desire to help irritated Otaro even further, because I suppose they took a form not unlike that of a small boy who wishes to be of assistance to his elders in what he perceives to be a particularly knotty game.

As Jingen worked at the food, Otaro put his back against a tree and sighed deeply while examining his nails and picking the dirt from beneath them with a small knife. I stretched myself against the nearest tree and began.

"We may not find her."

"True Captain, the ground is bad for the purpose, but perhaps with sufficient application…"

I shrugged at this. He was the tracker after all, but I began, "something has occurred to me and it's very curious."

"Go on, Captain."

"The footmarks by Master Sum's training ground, they were the marks of seven men, seven men who almost exactly correspond or so you tell me, in training and technique to the party that attacked and killed Lord Hoji".

"Lord Hoji took his own life, Captain; they did not kill him. But you are correct in the essentials."

"These men also bear a resemblance to those boys in white who attacked us on the first night after we left Lord Hoji's castle."

"In style, yes. There was the fellow of the Edo school and the Yakamaru practitioner."

"Men whom we are relatively certain we shot or cut down. And yet, how old are the marks on the beach?"

Otaro coughed and looked almost embarrassed at this question.

"Three days, four at the most, Robert."

"Does that not seem strange to you? Nine men, six of whom fall in the attack on Lord Hoji. You read it in the dust yourself when this whole queer business started. Three times we've fought them and every time some have fallen, how can it be that this company can come through four fights and only seem to lose two of their number, it's incredible!"

Otaro smiled at me and made an open handed gesture. "What are you suggesting Robert? That they are ghosts?"

At this I thanked the heavens that we had been conversing in English for I had no wish to send the otherwise admirable Jingen into another fit of the horrors.

"Don't be ridiculous, Otaro," I snapped, "but you must grant me that this is exceedingly strange."

"Then what are you suggesting, Robert? You know as well as I that our eyes deceive us, you've told me yourself that in battle not a shot in ten tells. The same is not true when the fighting is close, but still many a wounded man can fight on and there are often wounds that look worse then they are. My forehead", he pointed at the pink line of the wound, "proves the rule. But you're right, they can't be ghosts, they have feet."

I exploded at this, enraged that Otaro was not taking my concerns entirely seriously.

"Well of course they're not damn ghosts, man, but think of the other possibilities. Either they are preternaturally hardy men with the physiques of Hercules who are capable of shrugging off sword blows and bullets, or, and this is far more likely, they are not samurai."

At this Otaro sat bolt upright, regarding me keenly, his knife still in his hand, forgotten. "You said it yourself, that none of Lord Ide's men are up to the mark and Lord Hoji's men are all accounted for. What if the attackers were not samurai?"

"No, it is you who are being ridiculous, Robert. These are men of skill."

"Again, you said yourself, Master Sum is a fine teacher, would he not be capable of training such men?"

"He would, Robert, but think about what you are saying. Such skill is the product of a lifetime's training and for your assertion to be true, he would have to have trained at least twenty men. It is too incredible, it would take…"

"...years. When did he enter Lord Hoji's service?"

"Ten, maybe twelve years ago."

"There you are, take a boy of ten or twelve."

"No, no, no, much younger, Captain. Such skill would have to be nurtured from a very young age, six at least."

"And a six year old would be sixteen or eighteen now."

"But the men we killed were not boys, Robert."

"Maybe he took some older students."

"And trained them, a small army of them, secretly, with no word of it reaching anyone? This is insane, Robert. They are not samurai!"

"We know that, they murdered Jingen's family and ambushed a man on the way to christen his son."

"Christen?"

"The blessing of the waters, you understand. But hardly the acts of honourable men."

"True, but that is hardly the point, it is impossible, you cannot grow a flower from a bean seed, it is simply impossible."

And with that he threw up his hands and got to his feet. I stepped back as I realized that the conversation was growing heated and Jingen was standing nearby holding bowls of food and looking anxious that his masters were quarrelling. We took the bowls and began to eat with greater heartiness then either of us felt. The alternative was to begin the conversation again and

Otaro was too bruised in his prejudices to relish the prospect. I knew that he would never accept it. His sense of caste and propriety were too strong. The very idea that commoners might possess skill at arms was an affront. It was the old feudal problem again, a man could not be better than his birth. His station in life was as set from that moment as if it had been carved in stone. It was quite understandable that the aristocracy of nature, merit and God-given talent would rebel against such an archaic creed. That the peasant lads might wield a blade with as much skill as a Lord might discomfit Otaro, but it was a self evident truth and it was also the only explanation thus far that did not require us to descend to the mental level of idiots, requiring either ghosts or supermen to make sense of things.

Dinner done, we pushed on for another few hours, until we encountered our third stream. Otaro pronounced the situation hopeless and admitted that for several hours we had been advancing on little better than guess-work. It was an admirable declaration; he had failed, but was honest in admitting it, which characteristic elevated my friend over the common run of his race, who infinitely prefer a pleasant lie to an unpleasant truth[44]. I ventured that at least we were nearing the crest of the mountain and we would almost certainly be able to spot Lord Hoji's army from our elevated position. We could to make for it and inform him of his fencing master's crime with all due alacrity. Otaro seemed little comforted by this, though we had not spoken much since our argument. It was plain that he realized my logic was unassailable and it vexed him deeply. I did my best to be

---
[44] The Japanese can hardly be said to be alone in that.

magnanimous about it and held this course of action up as a peace offering. He took it with as much grace as he could muster and we resolved to make an all-out march for the crest the next morning in order to locate Lord Hoji's army and spy out the most expeditious route. Otaro took the first watch after some cajoling and we bedded down for the night.

Mine was the middle watch, and that was drawing to a close, when I heard a rustling in the undergrowth. With great care, I pushed my thumb against my scabbard, thus drawing my blade almost silently. The darkness in the trees was total, but for the faint glow of our dying fire and I strained my eyes to catch some shape or movement. Then I heard it again, not a tread or a footfall, but a whispering of leaves, whereupon I concluded that it was probably an animal. I did not want to wake my friends unnecessarily, but I needed to be sure. The movement was farther away now, very soft, more felt than heard, and my ears pricked. Willing my beating heart to be still, I followed it, turning with the sound as it circled our little camp. All was silent, but for the snores of my companions and the sighs of the sleeping horses. I made for the beasts as they were the obvious target of an assailant, though I was more than half convinced that what I heard was some nocturnal animal. Rocinante slept fitfully, shivering under her blanket, her eyes rolling beneath their lids. I put out a hand to quieten her and she stilled a little, when, as if a cloud had passed from the face of the moon, I saw the girl.

She was small and finely made, her skin more Chinese than Japanese, not exactly darker but richer like burnished gold.

Hers was not the complexion of a peasant's wife, but the full flushed tone of a woman of health and vigor. Every aspect of her appearance spoke of her restless vitality. Her form was slim and athletic, a girl in whom the spark of life burned fast and bright. She advanced from the trees, nearing the last embers of our fire and she tossed some dried grasses upon it. It flamed into life again. This exposed her fully to my eye and roused the sleepers. As Jingen and Otaro turned in their blankets, I marvelled at what the new light had revealed to me. She was clad in a simple robe of red that covered her from neck to foot, but her head and face were visible. But what a noble head! Her face was small and was as perfect a picture of beauty as can be thought of. Her nose was small, her chin strong, her lips full and her small eyes glittered in the firelight so dark as to appear almost black. But this was not her most striking characteristic, because she possessed something I have never seen in a Japanese woman from that day to this, her hair which was as delicately arranged as that of any lady of the court at Yeddo was a bright burnish flaming red. It was coiled about her head in the traditional style and caught the firelight so that it glowed as if it were of the fire itself.

I smiled and sheathed my sword immediately, before bowing to the lady. She returned my bow most prettily and I stepped forward to speak with her. A cry from beside me told me that the sleepers had awoken. I turned to see Otaro, rolling from his blanket, his sword in his hand, his face contorted into a violent attitude and his eyes wide with terror and surprise. I rushed to him and holding out my hand quietened him. He was so overcome he could not speak, his brow was dewy as if with fever and he twitched. Jingen likewise was much disturbed, his wide eyes looking over the edge of his blanket shone in the firelight and even the relative darkness could not conceal his trembling. Uttering soothing words to Otaro who seemed much exercised, I turned again to the lady.

"You must forgive my companions, madam, they were taken unawares," I said, desperate to put this fine woman, who had fled at our coming to Master Sum's at her ease. "But you have nothing to fear from us."

She bowed, her wide sleeves touching the ground as she did so.

"I know that Captain," said she, her voice beautiful, but having nothing light or of the girl about it. It was strong and clear, the voice of an adult woman in full possession of her power. I was forced to reappraise her. This was no servant and was perhaps Master Sum's wife or even daughter. I made to speak, but she raised her hand. "You have been following me for a long time now, Captain, and I regret I could not aid you sooner, but only in the last few hours have I been able to shake off my pursuers. I have done my best for you when I could, but my strength is coming to an end and I have to pass on the burden."

As you can imagine, I was much confused by this. That she was some relative of Master Sum's was clear, but as for her aiding us, I could not exactly understand it. Presumably she had interceded on our behalf with him. She knew me, though I had never laid eyes on her. I kept my voice as steady and amiable as

I could, having no wish to startle her, "Lady what is your name? If there is a burden of which we can relieve you, simply tell us. What are you to Master Sum?"

"Nothing but an enemy to him and his." She paused and spat the word. "His kind. My name is Mariko and the burden of which I speak is here."

She turned and I almost went after her lest we lose her in the trees. It is no small matter to find someone who does not wish to be found in a forest like that in the dark, but I hesitated lest in doing so I scared her and precipitated what which I wished to avoid. But I need not have feared. She stepped once more into the circle of firelight and our astonishment, she held in her arms a little bundle that stirred fitfully and extended a tiny hand to grasp at his covers. It was the lost heir.

She passed him to me and I confess I was in a daze. To have worked and striven for so long and to have the object of our quest handed to me, safe and alive after all this adventure was stunning. I am no great student of babies, but he seemed a pleasant little fellow, plump and red with health, eyes closed against the tumult of which he had been the cause, snuffling in his covers, lost to sleep. I was lost, struck dumb with surprise, when the lady stepped away for a second time and returned bearing a sword. It was a simple thing of black lacquer and well worn haft, but Otaro gasped at the sight of it. I knew them the truth of the matter. Here was the boy whom Lord Hoji had held to his bosom when all hands were turned against him and there was the blade that had served him. I passed the child to Otaro, who took him wordlessly, still agape. The lady Mariko, placed the sword of Lord Hoji, made by Plodding Saburo, given to him by Benkei and stolen from him by treachery and ambush into my hands.

"I put this child in your hands Captain, because I no longer have the strength to protect him and, the sword also. It was the true object of all this. You are a good man, Captain, and have in you a great deal of Jizo[45]. I pray you can take him home where I could not."

I nodded that I would, mesmerized by what had happened. I raised the sword to eye height and pushed it gently from its scabbard, drawing it forth. I saw the characters "Labour's Reward" engraved on the glistening steel, flashing in the firelight. I made to speak, to ask how it had all happened. How had she come by both sword and child, how had she kept them safe under the very nose of Master Sum? When I tore my eyes away from the sword, she was gone.

I ran into the trees, calling her. Otaro, finally coming to his senses, passed the child to Jingen and drew his sword, dashing after me. We ranged through the darkened forest, crying "Mariko!", barking our shins, tripping and falling in the dark, until it was clear that it was hopeless. Well may you smile, that a woman, particularly one in the constricting habit of a Japanese woman of rank would lose us, but it was no great thing to conceal yourself in a thick forest in the dark from two searchers. We gave it up after almost an hour. She could not but have heard us,

---

[45] A traditional Japanese deity whose special province is the protection of children.

it is almost impossible to find someone who does not wish to be found. I came back to the fire, to find Jingen sitting against a tree, with the baby resting on his lap, looking concerned but happy.

"Captain, Lord, he will be hungry when he wakes and we have nothing fit for a baby." I shrugged at this and asked Otaro who was bending in the undergrowth what he was about. It seemed too much to hope that he might track her. He replied that he had only found some animal tracks and that it was of no importance, though he seemed greatly discomfited as we made our way back to the fire. I gave it up and handed him the sword, which he obviously wished to examine. His aspect changed immediately at the prospect of handling such a masterpiece of the armourer's art. I was glad for his distraction. I cannot say I was wholly satisfied, but at the same time it seemed a low thing to me to pursue her who had handed us the means of discharging our oath to Lady Hoji, almost certainly at great cost to herself. I reproached myself for having attempted it and leaving Jingen to take watch and care for the child and Otaro enraptured by the blade in his hands, I lay down to sleep.

21

Travel with babies.
Return to the castle.
A rout.

I am not accustomed to babies, but it seems that, unlike a man, who can be induced to understand that short rations are his lot and, will submit quietly, a baby will have none of it. To be frank, the little fellow howled for hour upon ululating hour, pausing only to take great breathy gasps of air and then howl again. Otaro took it all stoically, but Jingen was right and the child, whose Christian[46] name I realized to my embarrassment I had not concerned myself to learn, would not be pacified. We were pushing onto the crest to get the lay of the land, when Jingen had an idea. He boiled some rice and fish together in a small pot for almost an hour, reducing them to a mush and fed the mixture to the child by taking it on his fingers and letting the child suck it from there, which quietened him.

I took the opportunity to speak to Otaro, for not-withstanding our need to get to the crest so that we could see what we were about, our plans would have to be revised in light of the extraordinary developments of the night before. Otaro who

---
46 I think we can safely say that here Captain Hood means given name.

looked drawn after the night's adventures was direct, "We have three things that must be accomplished. Firstly, we must return the child to his mother as we are sworn to do. Secondly, we must find and capture Master Sum. And thirdly, we must return Lord Hoji's sword to his heir."

I was surprised. Though Otaro was worn and his eyes had a little of the brightness of fever about them, he seemed more animated than before. He seemed to think that we might capture Master Sum. I told him.

He made a face.

"True, is it is not probable that the matter will go before any judge, but the possibility remains."

"You think he will run?" I asked.

"No, where could he run to? Also we have what he seeks, he will eventually find us, that is the way of such men."

And then I realized that he was right. That Master Sum would not sneak into the night like a Mexican desperado, but would come to us, and it was the coming confrontation that had so lifted my friend's spirits.

I felt we should move on as soon as we could, as I did not want to be caught by Master Sum and his band while we had the child. It would be cruel if the little fellow could survive the death of his father and nearly two months on the run only to be lost because we did not get him home quickly enough. With that in mind, I ordered Jingen to prepare as much of the fish mush as he could so that we would not have to stop to prepare more. Jingen was very taken with the lad and was as tender as any father could be, always talking to him in a sing-song voice as he fed, and sparing no pains to look to the child's comfort or security. He often referred to the baby as "Itatzi", a word which was unknown to me at the time, but which Otaro told me later meant something like weasel or ferret. As I had no other name for the boy other than this, somewhat odd, endearment, I took to using it myself. Otaro, was a little scandalized when I lent Jingen my horse and tried to dissuade me, but it seemed to me a little cruel that Jingen should have to walk and carry the precious object of our mission. Also it had a more practical object. If we were ambushed, he was to ride like the devil for Lord Hoji's castle and not to release the child except into the care of Lady Hoji herself. Otaro would not run in any case and I was disinclined to sacrifice Itatzi to his sense of honour.

We reached the crest about mid morning. The air was cool and the trees had thinned out to bursh and scrub before we reached the crest. Our view was unimpeded. The country was spread out around us like a blanket and I soon saw the point of getting to this height. Lord Hoji's castle was but the breadth of a valley distant. Two days march, one if we really pushed ourselves, and we would push. We forged on into the valley, travelling as quickly as we were able. Jingen asked if we could stop at one of the villages that dotted the valley floor, but I would have none of it. Itatzi might hunger for a day or two, but better by far to see him safe inside the walls of his uncle's castle. We kept a punishing pace up; Otaro and Jingen with the horses at the quick step and I forced marching till my thighs and calves ached, my feet blistered and my throat was dry as dust. We moved on until we reached the paddy fields and terraces of the valley floor and made one stop. The fields were empty, unsurprising given the talk of war, but we met a peasant woman with three children. She almost ran at the sight of us, but paused when she saw Itatzi, whom I supposed undermined any martial appearance. She was young and sturdy, not yet worn down by the travails of the peasant life. Her round face was burned nut brown by the sun, but was still pretty for all that. She had about her a look of determination coupled with the stoicism and humour that characterizes the Japanese peasant. Having seen us and coming to the conclusion that we were not raiders, she walked on, pulling two little girls behind and carrying the other, heading east whence we had come. Our road snaked through the paddy fields, until it reached the foot of the mountain, hers was separated from ours by a narrow paddy. She bowed as we passed, instructing her daughters (I could not guess their ages, but would have made the larger above knee height, five perhaps?) to do the same. We had passed each other then, when an idea came into my head, telling Otaro and Jingen to wait, I dashed across the bank of the paddy towards her. Her sudden understanding that I was not Japanese was clear, for she gaped in a mixture of terror and surprise and I think if she had been able, she would have run. Otaro and Jingen waited for me on the opposite bank, both men taking the opportunity to dismount and stretch their legs. It was funny to see the patrician Otaro and the plebian Jingen making the same squatting, stretching and hopping movements in an effort to rid themselves of their saddle soreness, neither of the two men would ever show a good leg on a horse and it showed in their discomfort.

I had reached the peasant woman who was bowing now for all she was worth and very much afraid to look me in the eye. The little girls were under no such anxiety and marvelled openly, until their mother put them to bowing again with a curt reproof. Her name I discovered was also Mariko, but I attached no importance to this curious coincidence.

"Where are you from, Mariko?" I asked.

"This village, Lord."

"And where are you going?"

"To my uncle's house, Lord."

"Where is everybody else?"

"I do not know, Lord"

We went on in this vein for several minutes, until I realized that nothing of use was going to be discovered from this woman. She was quite wisely on her guard, refusing to say anything that might damn her in the eyes of either faction. I despaired, but suddenly had an idea, that while it embarrassed me might overcome her reserve. I called Jingen over and then lacking the words to properly express my meaning in Japanese I had to ask her with my hands if she would feed little Itatzi for us. I produced two of the coins that Lord Hoji had given us for the road and she soon caught the idea. Jingen produced Itatzi, whom she cooed over briefly, then bared her breast and began the business. Women see little point in ceremony when there are babies to be fed. I retired at this point more for my blushes than for hers and left her talking to Jingen, who was holding forth effusively on Itatzi, his manly qualities, his strength and so forth. As I retired, I noticed that her diffidence vanished and she became quite haughty with poor Jingen, recognizing no doubt some sign of his lowly caste invisible to my "ignorant" western eyes.

Jingen returned twenty minutes later with a sleeping Itatzi cradled in his arms, having obviously bored poor Mariko to tears with the superlative qualities of this prince amongst babies, but as I thought he was shrewd enough in his way.

"There is news, Lord. There is an army marching here."

"No, marching on Lord Ide's castle surely."

"No, Lord, that army is retreating back to the castle of blood."

"Has there been a battle then?"

Now even Otaro was pricking up his ears.

"No, Lord, but the army has driven Lord Hoji's army back. It is a new army with guns from Yeddo."

"From Yeddo?"

"Truly, Lord, Lord Ide's men were joined by an army from Yeddo. They are terrible men and crush everything in their path."

Otaro looked aghast at this, "An army from Yeddo can only mean that the people of consequence have decided to side with Ide. My message must have arrived too late. The army must have been dispatched before it was received."

Then as if to give life to our thoughts, there was a crash of cannon in the distance, followed by a rippling crackle of musketry from down the valley.

"It seems battle is joined, then," said Otaro, who seemed somewhat dazed by the prospect.

"Well then, we had better hurry, if we are to discharge our oath."

That shook him from his daze and we marched on, adopting now an even more punishing pace. Noon passed and we began to see the first stragglers like dots in the distance, growing clearer as we and they neared Lord Hoji's castle. They flew without weapons, their armour gone, blackened by sweat and powder smoke.

"Lord Hoji has lost, it seems." said Otaro gravely.

"Probably, but not for certain. All battles look like this from the rear, whether you win or lose, though I can't say I'm much saddened by the prospect of him losing. He's a murderous fellow. Just ask Jingen."

Otaro obviously found this attitude odd, because we spoke no more that day but only marched on until we neared the castle as the sun began to set.

The valley was alive with fugitives. Far off there were pillars of smoke stretching up into the sky where somewhere a village was burning. A horseman galloped past us, flogging his beast to death in the effort to escape. Blood flecked foam flew from her mouth and I recognized the rider as one of Kaneda's cronies, now pale with terror rather than with paint. We called to him, but he went on unheeding. The light had not yet begun to fade when I heard the first volley crashing down the valley, I turned to look and saw formed bodies of men advancing several miles from us. I thought, almost believed, that I saw the Major at the head of one of them, standing high in the stirrups and shouting orders as Lord Hoji's rear guard of horsemen menaced the advancing columns. The footsoldiers fired, a few fell and the horse soldiers broke off again, only to repeat the procedure a few minutes later. There were other men moving across the crisscross of dykes and banks that divided the paddy fields. They wore an unfamiliar livery and had little of the drill of Lord Hoji's troops, but they rolled on just the same. The valley was dotted with bodies now; the wounded succumbing to their injuries, the fatigued giving into exhaustion and throwing themselves on the ground in despair. It was a rout.

We reached the castle, as the sun was sinking in the West and the mountainside, sky and all were suffused with a deep burning red. I have seen the same effect in the Arizona territory when I was hunted by a pack of vengeful Apache in the Sangre de Christos mountains, but that did not move me as this did. Men were crawling, dying on the road to the castle, shedding armour and pride as they went. Dragging shattered limbs and maimed comrades, they struggled onwards, these men who had only discovered this morning the deadly truth of the Minie ball. As we came to the gates of the castle, we passed a man lying face down in a brackish puddle by the side of the road. He was a young man and tall, his legging wet and his armour rent where the bullets of the enemy had pierced it. His hair, which had come undone, was long and lay on the surface of the water, the long strands moving sluggishly caught in the cloud of dark blood that spread slickly across the water. We splashed past him and as we entered beneath of the arch of the gate, the courtyard already thronged with the lost, I looked up and saw the castle as the sun set behind it. The centre of a red mass that enfolded us all, spreading across the sky like the flow from a new wound.

22

Duty done.
A terrible understanding.
The duel in the tower.

The castle was in the grip of a total and overwhelming chaos. The elegant manse usually the home of ease and nicety was overcome by catastrophe. The central courtyard was thronged by a mass of soldiers, wounded or terrified. Some still clung to their weapons and dignity, but most were utterly lost. Otaro and I had to beat a path through the press with our scabbarded swords before we made any headway. There was plenty of space in the many gardens further back in the castle grounds, but the crowd would not move from the main courtyard and the weak and the injured were trampled. As we passed through it I saw some of the older men and the chamberlain tearing down part of a doorway with pikes to encourage the mob to move. The white faced boy who had galloped past us outside the castle, lay on the steps, his head in his hands and subject to such a profound despair that when the soldiers finally began to move, he was only dislodged from the steps by kicks. A sallow faced man beside me called for water. An archer, his face opened by a sword blow, wept blood and tears. We passed through the doorway as quickly as we could into the garden beyond. There, doctors in their strangely shaped hats were passing out water from a great wooden tun[47] and plastering the wounded with bandages of translucent paper. We dismounted and taking the child, left Jingen to hold the horses lest they be stolen from the stables. Otaro took the lead and we walked across the green sward now stained with crimson, stepping between crushed flowers in search of a servant who could lead us to Lady Hoji. The place smelled of defeat, of fear, of blood and bowels laid open to the air.

It was curious. They had none of the anger of a defeated army. The castle was quiet enough beyond the occasional cries for water. The only sound left was the shuffling of feet and of many bodies breathing. It was as if, having been defeated, the bravado of the samurai deflated like a balloon and all was silence and despair. Even the wounded were muted. A servant passed by, his face ashen and his hands red to the elbows with someone else's blood. Otaro grabbed him by the arm, but the man merely shrugged him off and Otaro and I exchanged looks, knowing that to pursue him would have been useless. Otaro moved back and forth trying to stop someone, anyone, to convey us to Lady Hoji, but it was futile, so we began to search the castle ourselves. Night fell and a cannon boomed in the distance, but the musket fire grew ever closer as we moved through the labyrinth of square boxlike rooms calling Lady Hoji's name. Cries and yells arose from the outside and were followed by a thunder of hooves and we knew that Lord Hoji had returned from the scene of his

---

47 A type of large wooden barrel or tub.

defeat. The castle was not large, but I soon became lost in the unending white paper rooms, gardens and then more rooms again. I forgot which walls were walls and which were doors and simply followed Otaro. There was a great yell again from the courtyard and it seemed as if Lord Hoji was rallying his troops, but then we heard firing again.

It was wild fire, ragged and not the sharp crash of musketry that I had come to associate with Major Fitzpatrick's well drilled men, but the enemy were without, to be sure, and the battle would soon begin in earnest. Such was the shambles the castle had descended to that we could not find one single servant who had seen Lady Hoji or could tell us where she could be found. It was as if some fine and complex machine had been smashed almost to pieces, leaving parts of the mechanism still ticking uselessly. We had been directed to the ornamental pond by a serving girl where I had first met Master Sum who had said that would find Lady Hoji there, when we met Lord Hoji. His helmet was off and his hair had come undone and it clung about his massive brow, matted with sweat and blood. His armour bore the mark of the enemy clearly. As he strode across the garden, ordering what few men remained him to the walls, his eyes meet ours and he stopped. Those who walked about him kept moving to their appointed places, but he was absolutely still. Otaro bowed and I did also and a rocket arched into the air, staining everything with a sickly yellow light as he acknowledged the courtesy. His teeth, several of which were newly broken and rimed with blood gleamed in the glare of the rocket as he smiled.

Otaro moving with a studied slowness took Itatzi from my arms and offered him to Lord Hoji.

"Your cousin Lord, I return him to you."

A panicked samurai rushed at Lord Hoji bleating for orders, but the man silenced him with a wave of his hand and lifted the little lad, holding him up so that his legs dangled and the child kicked a little. It was extraordinary, his hair wild and his armour splattered with blood smiling at the child. It was as if our poor fellow who had died in the puddle at the castle gates had risen and was now looking at his younger self, who stared at him, innocent and uncomprehending of what was to come.

"He is well, a fine strong boy. Who had him?" He said, not sparing us a glance, unable to tear himself away from the child.

"Master Sum, Lord. He also had your uncle's sword."

He cut a look at us. "Master Sum, are you sure?"

"Beyond all doubt, Lord"

"Well we shall have to look for him," he indicated with a nod the tumult outside, "after this." Two of his samurai stood by him, their eyes a silent plea to be led, but he ignored them. "Could you bring these things to my aunt," he added quietly and Otaro bowed again. "Thank you, thank you both," he said and then he was gone, shouting, exhorting, threatening amidst the chaos. I was quite moved by his display of sang froid and though I could never forget the terrible deeds that he had been author of, he was magnificent that night. He was a great, terrible man, or a terrible great man; I am still uncertain myself of the truth of it.

But we were still in the some dilemma, where was Lady Hoji? Yamagatsi was hard on the heels of his chief, the battle had spared him, thank God, for he was a kind man. He was leading a squad of archers, almost all of them wounded, to the walls, when Otaro stopped him. Lady Hoji was in the tower at the rear of the castle, he said quickly, nodding to me and most incongruous of all, pausing to coo and wave at Itatzi in my arms. Another rocket shrieked overhead and we ran for the tower, where already musketeers and archers were taking their places to pour fire at the enemy. Splinters flew overhead as they were lashed by volleys from without and more than one fell as we rushed in. Here at least there was order, samurai and men at arms making for the top of the tower while servant girls moved through the halls, now dark, now shot through with the flaring light of rockets, silent and swift on unknowable errands. We mounted the stairs and came to the level, just below the top floor. Otaro stopped one with a word and then we had our guide. The firing was incessant now, but the girl led us to her mistress, heedless of the shot that rent the walls around her, pausing only to stamp on a piece of smouldering debris that fell from the rafters above.

Lord Hoji's widow knelt in state before an audience of her serving women, her countenance as steady and imperturbable as that of a Roman statue. A ceremony was taking place, I knew not what, but she had a low table in front of her upon which there lay several sheets of paper, a brush, ink and a grindstone as well as several other articles and a brazier. Two of her maids held flowers and looked up when we were announced. I suddenly became aware that I was wearing my shoes indoors for the first time in months. The idea seized me so strongly that when I was presented to Lady Hoji I was bereft and incapable of anything. Otaro touched me gently on the elbow and I started. We advanced, bowed and knelt before Lady Hoji in our turn, one of the serving women having cleared away the things in front of her.

"Lady," said Otaro simply, "we wish to return to you your son who was taken from you and whom your husband died to save."

He indicated the child and a maid lent forward and took little Itatzi from me and placed him in his mother's arms. She softened and the cool beauty, which had so impressed me on our first meeting, was overcome by a flush of maternal feeling which banished all reserve. She smiled and offered him her fingers which he sucked and grasped at. A shudder passed through the assembled maids as an archer died screaming without, but Lady Hoji was as deaf as if she had been at the bottom of an ocean.

"Thank you sirs, for returning my son to me, I thank you," and she smiled at me with a look of genuine affection. Otaro bowed and I did likewise, then remembering what else had been taken, I offered her "Labour's Reward". She looked up from the child.

"Your son's inheritance", I said "and the cause of it all, for it was for this that Master Sum murdered your husband lady." Her expression changed, "Well it is his son's patrimony now", she replied, becoming grave. "Did he flee or did you kill him?"

Otaro cut me off. "Alas, he escaped lady, but he is a marked man and will not be able to hide for very long."

She heard this in silence and passing Itatzi to one of her maids, she bowed to us very deeply.

"Sirs, I thank you for all that you have done for me and regret that I may not be able to reward you as you deserve." At this I took the lead and Otaro be damned.

"You are most welcome, lady; the honour of doing you a service is honour enough. But if I may offer you another, the castle is not yet surrounded and we can still bring you and your son out."

Otaro stiffened at my side, but that gracious lady smiled. "Thank you Sir, but that will not be necessary, though I do appreciated your kindness." I began again, but she was politely obdurate and Otaro thoroughly embarrassed. It seemed that the samurai code of never showing your back was deeply held and not to be cast aside even by their womenfolk.

"Thank you", she said again and I felt Otaro's hand under my arm. We were dismissed.

We passed through several rooms until we reached the balcony overlooking the walls. Balls whizzed and popped around us and the night was bright with rockets and torches. To our right a begrimed archer lit fire arrows from a pot and sent them arching high into the sky to thud into the masses below. Hundreds of men were gathered around the walls, Lord Ide's and the troops from Yeddo in ranks back from the ramparts. There would be no escalade, they had no ladders, but there was a steady booming from the castle gates as they tried to force them only to be shot down by the defenders in the gate house. I saw a congregation of gallant hats standing by, watching as the assembled men tried to sweep the walls with volleys. The light glittered on the hundreds of brandished swords and spears, but I saw neither Lord Ide or Major Fitzpatrick. A small man in elaborate armour, whose helmet was marked with a massive crest, and who was surrounded by other lesser men gave orders with a fan. I could hear his stentorian voice even over the gun fire. More arrows flew and the ball flicked around us again.

"So this is what a battle looks like, Captain Robert. It seems so simple when one is not in it," said Otaro leaning on the rail.

"Why did you not let me take her, Otaro," I began, more in sorrow than in anger. "They will bring cannon soon and it will be all over. But there will be a great deal of killing first and round shot does not discriminate. Better we take her out and conduct her to their camp, than that she run the risk of being killed or worse, before she is taken. I am sure you could make her listen to reason. Or at least even if we cannot get her out, we could stand guard over her. Sieges even short ones, are very cruel and it will not be well for her to be here without protection."

We moved back from the rail then, not wishing to expose ourselves needlessly, now that Otaro had satisfied his curiosity.

"But she will not be taken, Captain Robert, none of them will," he said, looking at me quizzically.

"What do you mean?" I said, a sudden heaviness in my stomach. Otaro smiled patiently, "they cannot be taken, Captain, the shame would be too unbearable. I have suffered it once and only because I was taken insensible and without the means of ending my shame."

My understanding was sudden and my horror total.

"But what of the boy, what of him, mustn't she stay alive for him?"

And at this he patted my arm kindly, as if trying to comfort a child. "She will not let him dishonour the memory of his forebearers, Captain. She will be courageous for them both."

I ran, suddenly and without thinking, thundering across the floorboards like a man possessed. All I could think of was her kind terrible smile and the glittering straight bladed knife that I had seen by her brushes when we had entered. "You're mad," I screamed. I already saw the knife descending, the little shriek, the muffled cry. Otaro ran after me, catching at my arm. I shook him off and ran down the corridor, my heart hammering in my chest, Otaro after me. I rushed to the door, as a chorus of feminine screams rang above the clamour of battle. I reached the doorway, already convinced of the worst when my breath was taken away by the scene that greeted me.

Master Sum stood across the room his face ugly with hatred. He was dirty and travel-stained, his wispy hair in disarray. He dashed at Lady Hoji, reaching for the sword that had been so long denied him and for whose possession he had murdered his Master and plunged two princedoms into bloody war.

"Give it me, you whore," he howled as he came at Lady Hoji, who knelt before her son, a knife in her hand. The room was a sea of bodies, terrified maids and ladies in waiting, rushing about, pushing past us, tearing at each other and sometimes at themselves. A brazier was knocked over and a lick of flame rushed up the eastern wall of the chamber. It seemed that some instincts are stronger than others, for Lady Hoji, all thoughts of suicide gone, plucked up Itatzi and made to get away.

We pushed against the crowd when the first high pitched scream and spurt of blood told me that Master Sum was cutting a path to his prize. The heat hurt my eyes now, as the room filled with smoke and the panic grew and the girls stampeded past us. There was a tearing sound and above the crush of little bodies, I saw a white clad figure with eyes dark as death step through the paper wall behind Lady Hoji. He swung at her, his sword held high for a killing stroke that would have split her in two, when she turned suddenly without seeing the man and buried her blade in his brain. She staggered back, her face paler than ever. But it was when she saw Master Sum snatch up "Labour's Reward" that the tigress awoke within her, the gift of her noble line, and she scorned him for a coward and a thief, her voice shrill above the tumult. Otaro had been less delicate than I, beating a way through the crowd with the flat of his scabbard and was closer. I heard the first death gurgle where he did not.

I turned to see two young men, clad all in white, swords drawn and murder in their eyes standing over the body of a maid from whose tiny body there flowed an impossibly large quantity of blood. They were white, so incredibly pale as to be actually white, not white as you or I, but white as a sheet of paper, so that the flames that were engulfing the room almost seemed to flicker through them. They were unruffled by the slaughter. No excitement or frenzy of battle showed in their dark eyes. They simply swept forward, as if they were at their exercises. I had drawn my sword already and lunged forward to give the fellow on the left the point through the bowels. It is a maneuver unknown in Japanese fencing, but it discomfited his companion not a bit. My man fell, his sword clattering on the hard wood floor and moved no more, but his fellow cut at me savagely, advancing quickly and unleashed such a volley of blows that I lost my feet trying to get away from them. I rolled out of the way, then scuttled like a crab to get to my feet again. He would have had me, if he had pressed, but he stopped to cut down a girl who was running in circles around the room, lost in the smoke and the fire. His recovery was rattlesnake fast, but not fast enough as I gave him a cut across the eyes that blinded him and then hacked him down with a two handed stroke that would have done Otaro proud. I looked back into the chamber, to see it full of smoke and flame and death.

Master Sum's students poured through the flaming walls unconcerned by the shimmering heat. Otaro felled one and then another, his body a blur, becoming like a sword of wind, whistling, deadly and never seen until it had come to a shuddering halt in another man's flesh. Lady Hoji tried to flee, her son in one arm, his birthright in the other. Master Sum, that terrible old man, carved a bloody way to her through the bodies of her fleeing serving women. Her face was that of a fury as she ducked behind pillars and dodged falling debris.

"Coward! Traitor!" she cried.

"Drop the sword, drop the sword, save the child, he only wants the sword." I yelled after her as I rushed to intercept Master Sum. I do not know, I shall never know, if she heard me because at that moment the demoniacal fencing master appeared over her and she fell to the floor to avoid the first blow, but not the second. That noble lady turned her body, curling it about her son as she lay. The wretch's blade cut her to the bone. It rose and fell like a woodman's axe. I could barely see through the smoke, but I knew it was all over for her.

Sum had bent to pick up the blade, when he jerked suddenly, swinging it up to block a strike from Otaro, who pushed him back across the body of the woman he'd cut down. The Master countered, whipping forward, catching Otaro's sleeve and dragging him off balance, long enough for him to bring his blade to bear. I was deafened by the roaring of the blaze and the heat haze made the two whirling figures swim before my eyes, as I toiled through the smoke, thick and choking now, to reach the poor lady's body. I staggered forward on my hands and knees, wincing as a stray ball, from the battle outside, whistled through the floor and clipped my thigh. Over the crackle of the fire, I thought I heard the boom of cannon, but could not know for sure. I reached her body, still curled around little Itatzi, her face strangely peaceful in terrible contrast to the wound on her back, the flesh laid bare to the bone. I rolled her over and brought out the child who was howling, his face a red mask, tracked with tears. He wept for he knew not what, though he still had a great deal to weep for. I made for the door, limping now and I could feel the blood running into my brogan when I was caught in a terrible dilemma. I must save the child, but I couldn't abandon my friend to the terrible fencing master alone. Otaro was renowned, but this man was one of the most terrible swordsmen of his day.

Then a roundshot crashed through the walls, carrying with it a mighty wind that swept the smoke in circling eddies and revealed to me the sight of Otaro and Sum, facing each other as if on the dueling field. They bowed and took up their stances once more. More shot flew through the tower and I coughed and spluttered through the smoke as the two figures erupted into furious action. Sum attacked, his blade ringing in killing blows, each of which Otaro danced out of by a hair's breadth. My friend was driven back desperately parrying, dodging, throwing all his resolve into defence, fighting for his life. Each time he would escape death by a fraction and attempt a riposte only to be overcome by the lightning fury of the fencing master's blows. The smoke parted about them, curling as the wind caught it. But Otaro kept his poise mastering himself where a thousand would have lost their heads and died in a second. He fought for life with a cool studied brilliance as the Master hurtled forward, feeding his rage into his swordplay, fighting as a much younger man would, trying to overcome by sheer speed and anger. Otaro let him press forward and, parrying for the tenth time in as many seconds, sidestepped quickly and directed a vicious cut at the Master. I saw the edge bite home and the blood flowed from the left arm of Sum's kimono, but it bought Otaro nothing but a few seconds. The older man cooled suddenly as if reminded of his own mortality and neatly slipped Otaro's second blow. Otaro pressed the attack, but each strike came back at him, leaving him open to ever more cunning counter attacks. It was as if injury had flensed the fury from Master Sum's soul. He was cool now and twice as deadly and he now bent every aspect of his art to Otaro's destruction. My friend was on the defensive again, fighting for his life amidst the smoke and chaos, while I wasted precious seconds caught between saving Itatzi or aiding my friend.

My choice was made for me, when lurching through the smoke came a figure of living fire. It was awful and there were no screams, but the man whose white kimono and hair burned like a roman candle came at Otaro, his sword held forward, cutting at him in eerie silence. I quickly placed Itatzi on the ground and dashed to Otaro's aid. He was backing away again, easily dodging the clumsy blows of the flaming man, but in doing so losing precious moments to defend against Master Sum. I scrambled across the chamber, my lungs aching with the smoke, tripping over a fallen beam, to strike at the burning figure. It was a low blow, but it was two against one and there was nothing else for it. I slashed him across the back and he fell suddenly, turning as he did so to grasp at my leg. He must have been at the very extremity of life for his fingers were but charred stumps and burned my flesh. My leg buckled, the heat was so intense. It seemed terribly cold to the touch, like the grip of Charon himself. I looked up stunned by the fall to see Otaro knocked to the ground by a villainous kick only to realize that my friend had been gravely injured. His robes were slashed with blood and he lay panting on his back, his sword held high as Master Sum stood over him simply waiting to deliver the final blow. But it had already fallen and I had not seen it.

For in falling, Otaro had caught his man on an almost lunge, scything through Master Sum's garments and deep into his vitals. The old fencing master stood uncomprehending, clutching the sword he had sacrificed so much to win. He raised it to deliver the coup de grace to my fallen friend and his bowels slipped out from beneath his belt. Otaro did not flinch, but met it with open eyes and a stout heart, or would have, had not Jingen leapt through the smoke to hammer Master Sum from his feet. He clung to the teacher's back like a monkey, pumping Lady Hoji's dagger into the man's flesh, again and again and again.

23

Endings.

Otaro was gone, I feared dead, when I pulled myself to my feet and staggered over to him, unsteady with wounds and grief. But he lived. We all did. His body, though pale as any of Master Sum's students and breathing only faintly, still had life in it when I pulled Jingen from Master Sum and directed him to carry my friend. The cannon were firing every minute now and with each shot that crashed home, resistance grew weaker and yet more desperate. Lord Hoji was driven from his last refuge with those warriors still left him and died underneath the willow tree by the pond I had so admired on my first stay at the castle.

I visited it in the days after and one could still see the bullet pocks fresh in the bark. Lady Hoji, Master Sum and all his mysterious students perished atop their own funeral pyre when the tower collapsed moments after Jingen and I had made our escape. The castle burned fiercely in the night, sparks rushing up towards the stars, the flames reflecting off the smoke that climbed ever upwards. I have never seen the sack of a city or even a town, but I imagine Soddom and Germorrah looked much like that which I saw that night. We were captured going over the wall by a band of Lord Ide's soldiers, though as luck would have it they recognized me as a foreigner and brought me straight away to Major Fitzpatrick. His foreign birth barred him from being in at the kill by order of Lord Ide and so he directed the cannonade at those parts of the castle still held by Lord Hoji's men. He was as merry and ferocious as ever, stripped to his shirt sleeves and with his bellicose beard shining in the fire light and his sword belt wrapped around his braces. He walked from gun to gun, taking his cigar out of his mouth only to curse the crews and damn them for a purblind mob of ignorant monkeys. He was as magnanimous in victory as he was terrible in battle and he had water brought for Otaro. Soon the castle was full of Lord Ide's and government troops and the cannon fire was stopped and he was idle.

"We'd given you up for dead, old fella. Glad to see you made it, damned if I know how."

His feeling was genuine and touched me to the heart, so that when he paused and said "Smoke?", offering me a cigar from his pocket, I could not speak, only nod. He smiled indulgently, "Good man, Robert, but keep your head down, you're lucky enough to make it this far, but the orders have been given for no prisoners on this job, you're lucky the lads brought you to me first, otherwise they'd have done for the lot of you, you, your pal, the fencing fella, who's quite genuine. The chaps from Yeddo were quite clear on that point, and that queer little orderly of yours."

It was then that I that saw the samurai emerging from the gates, heads hanging from their hands like so many oranges in a bag. "No prisoners?" I stammered, "why not?" "Carthago delenda something illy a jacta est, you know" he said, "something like that. Carthage must be destroyed. Condition of service, old boy, Lord Hoji disgraced himself and caused a horrid fuss, so the whole mob have to go, root and branch. They'll let the commoners go of course, but all the old house have to go. Then they can pretend the whole thing never happened. All must be put to the sword and not a stone left standing upon another."

And so it was. And in the camp by the castle where we nursed Otaro back to health the earth was continually rent by explosions as the ancient castle was blasted apart, rock by ancient rock. He was feverish all that time, the sheen of sweat on his pudgy little body making the thin paper bandages translucent like an image almost caught on a tintype, his livid scars eloquent testament to Master Sum's great, but imperfect skill. I stayed with him nights when it was worst and he was too sick to move. He babbled in dreams and nightmares: magic swords, castles, wars, princesses, foxes, ghosts, white ghosts coming to get him and death himself as an old man, and another who was death, but aflame and with dark eyes. They were lonely nights, though not without interest as I learned something of how Otaro saw our adventures and Major Fitzpatrick kept my company. He had been dismissed immediately after the battle, another of Yeddo's demands on Lord Ide. The great man himself took no interest in us, once a warrant establishing Otaro's credentials was received. My own position had also been somewhat precarious, since I had leave to travel in the interior only by his say so. With it of course came another warrant requiring me to be conveyed to Yokohama or one of the other treaty ports as soon as possible. This I refused to do until Otaro was well enough to be moved.

It was a three-week fever and during that time, I saw the destruction of Lord Hoji's castle in all its beauty. I observed that not all seemed well between the government forces, drawn from the personal armies of the other Lords, and Lord Ide himself, but that interested me little enough. It was late one morning, just before noon, when Edward and I were about to go for a short walk, when Suki ran to us, calling that Otaro was awake. We rushed into the temporary sickroom and saw him sitting up, very pale and greatly worn, but very much alive. We congratulated him and gave him a little soup, whereupon he fell asleep again. Several weeks passed and he became stronger, thinner than he had been and more wan, but still the same indomitable Otaro. Repeated demands for my removal came from Yeddoo, until the local commander would brook no more insolent refusal on my part and said that I would be on my way if he had to bind and gag me and put me on the horse himself.

The night before my departure, I stayed up with Otaro and we spoke of many things. His round face cracked a smile that shall forever remain in my memory, so unlike his usual acerbic self it was, but then he became serious.

"He was a fine swordsman, Captain, the best I have ever met. It was a terrible shame."

I did not feel it such a shame, Sum was a murderous villain, but I did not contradict Otaro on this. "That he should have done such things!" he shook his head. "He wanted to be the greatest and he was. I only beat him through fortunate circumstance, but that he should have done such things, he was mad."

"Mad with greed."

"Yes, for the sword of course, but it would have made no difference. A sword is but a sword. He would have always been the best. What happened in the end, Captain? I should like to know."

"It was lost with Master Sum and Lady Hoji when the tower collapsed."

"Lost like his students you mean? And their swords?"

"Just so."

"But they are picking through the rubble though are they not?"

"They are, but none of them are any use, they're all mangled by the heat, they're useless."

"And Labour's Reward?"

"No one has found it yet, it must have melted in the heat. You should have seen the place come down, it was like a furnace afterwards. They couldn't go near it for days."

He smiled weakly.

"Well that's good," and lay back on the pillows, "I shall stay here though, until all ten are found and disposed of appropriately."

I smiled at this, this peculiar foible of his, but I was tiring him and it would be an early start in the morning. We shook hands, a custom that always amused him and I rose to go. I had made my farewells and was almost at the door, when he called out to me.

"It was a pity about little Hoji, Captain, he would have been a great man like his father."

"It was a pity indeed, Otaro, I'm sure he would." I said.

It was the only time that I told my friend a deliberate untruth and though it rests ill with my conscience, the alternative would have been worse still. I had given little Itatzi into Jingen's care, mounted him on Rocinante and told him to ride like the devil and never look back. I think of them both often and hope they are well. I gave him Labour's Reward too, as it was Itatzi's only remaining inheritance, though I suppose she is probably buried or sold somewhere by now, as the son's of charcoal burners have very little use for swords.

FIN.

AUTHOR BIOGRAPHY

Conrad Kinch was born with the gift of laughter and the sense that the world was mad. He was variously employed in the Church, the book trade, newspapers and tourism. A poor hand with a sabre and an only passable pistol shot, he is fondly remembered by all those who have never lent him money.

He lives and works as a police officer in his native Dublin with his exceptionally patient wife, Mrs. Kinch, and two very demanding cats. His two children, Matilda and Edward, are auditioning for roles as villains in his next novel, which he will write after he's managed to get some sleep.

Made in the USA
Columbia, SC
08 March 2018